To S
W

Jacqui & the
Team BHR87·7
X

It Happened in Essex

Basildon Writers' Group

ISBN 9798686169692

Cover design and typo: publishingbuddy.co.uk
Editorial: Wendy Ogilvie Editorial Services

BHR 87.7 FM

This anthology is dedicated to Basildon Hospital Radio which is run by volunteers but, unlike other NHS volunteers running the shops, teas bars and help stations, you never see them. Yet they are the people who produce programmes of music to suit all tastes, chat about issues of the day, interview local people and provide a 24/7 service to transmit messages of love into and out of the hospital.

Despite having to leave their studio in the hospital when Covid 19 struck, BHR volunteers worked hard to reinvent themselves into a virtual radio station, and they have kept to their 24/7 promise to patients, staff and visitors.

But, one important problem remained; they could no longer do the fundraising so essential to even the most voluntary organisation.

Many of our writers have read their stories on BHR and we now have a chance to repay that hospitality, and recognise their amazing work in overcoming the problems not of their making. All payments from this book will be paid directly from Amazon to BHR, and we are proud to be able to use our imaginations and craft to help in a practical way

Contents

Part one

Part Two

A Fractured Fairy Story:
begun by Dawn Knox and completed by all writers.

The Witch and Sno White live in Basildon in 2020, and both want to be the Wednesday Presenter on the local radio station. Follow the hilarious imaginations of each writer, as they devise increasingly outlandish ways to resolve the dilemma, and win your vote for the most entertaining ending.

About the Writers

PART ONE

A Perfect Fit – Dave O'Neill ©

The tension was too much for Karen.

Closing the bedroom door to seek some welcome solitude, she heard the muted conversations from the girls downstairs fade as the door clicked shut behind her. She loved having the girls over, especially when they brought the grandchildren with them but, today, she just needed peace and quiet, and only the bedroom could provide that.

Karen sat on the edge of the bed, the tall mirror on the wardrobe door showing a well dressed but tired, middle aged woman, with dark hair that was tied back from her face. She could see the signs that she was starting to go slightly grey as her reflection stared back at her. She patted ineffectually at her hair for a second, smoothing an unruly wave back into place, only for it to spring back again. With a sigh she gave up and reached over to pull the wardrobe door open, looking at all his clothes as they hung lifeless in front of her. She had already decided that she would donate what she could to charity and knew that she had to make a start sorting them out sometime, but she also knew it wouldn't be easy. Standing up from the bed, she moved forward and started to pull the suits along the rail they hung on, mentally cataloguing those that she thought would be suitable for donating. Then, at the back, tucked away behind all the suits, she saw a zipped-up plastic cover. She frowned, thinking that she knew every item of clothing that he wore but, for some reason, she didn't know about this. Intrigued, she took it off the rail and, holding it up so she could see it in the light, unzipped it, gently pulling out what was inside. Thin tissue paper was wrapped around it which only added to the mystery. Carefully, so as not to rip the tissue paper, she exposed what was hidden beneath. For a second, she just stared blankly at what she held and then, with a gasp, the memories came flooding back, and she suddenly found herself reliving the moment she'd first seen this item of clothing, some thirty five, or more, years ago …

****

The sun dripped like molten gold from a sapphire sky as the coach finally came to a rest, the roar from the diesel engine dying at long last. Karen stretched her legs and looked out of the window, the sea a flat grey-blue, flecked with white. The staff summer outing of Basildon Biscuits was always talked about by the old hands in the factory and, as this was Karen's first time, she was really looking forward to it, but so far it hadn't got off to a good start. Billy, her boyfriend, was with his mates at the back of the coach, and Lisa, her closest friend, was stuck beside their boss, a few seats away. Karen had ended up sitting beside one of the delivery lads and she'd done her best to politely ignore him. He wasn't much fun anyway, his head in a book for the whole way there.

Karen wanted to get out and in to the fresh air as the smell of the cigarette smoke from those in the back seats was almost overpowering. The journey to the beach at Southend on Sea wasn't a long one and the atmosphere on the coach was almost party-like, though she felt a little left out.

'Here we are folks,' the driver called back down the smoke-filled aisle. 'Southend sea front. Now remember,' he said, 'we're leaving at half three so make sure you're all back out of the pubs, otherwise you'll be getting the train back to Basildon on your own.' The crowd at the back had cheered when they heard the word pub, drowning out anything else the driver was saying so he shook his head in defeat, laughed, and pulled the lever to open the big swing door at the front. 'Out, the lot of you,' he said waving them out the door.

As Karen worked her way down the aisle, Lisa jostled through to stand by her side.

'I thought I'd never get away,' Lisa whispered, faking a yawn and giving a tiny tilt of her head back to where their boss was still sitting. 'How was your journey down, then?' she asked.

Karen checked who was nearby, and whispered back, 'I was stuck with mister personality, one of the van drivers, for the whole journey, his head buried in a book.' she said. Not that she'd made any effort to engage him in a conversation, she thought, but that wasn't the point.

'A book? What, a man who can read?' and Lisa put on a mock shocked expression that Karen found herself smiling at. 'And were all the pictures coloured in!' They both laughed loudly at the joke, Karen sneaking a guilty look back towards – what was his name? – but she couldn't see him. He must be in the queue waiting to get off, she thought.

'Oi, Kaza, what you laughing at, girl?' someone shouted from the back. It was her boyfriend, Billy. He made some sort of comment to his mates and they all laughed. 'I'll see you outside, Kaza, alright?' he finished.

'I don't know why you're with him,' Lisa said, not looking back to where Billy and his gang were.

Karen shrugged. 'He asked me out so I said okay.' It wasn't like she found herself in demand, being small and having a shock of jet-black hair that wouldn't do anything she

3

wanted. Even the hair-band she wore to hold her hair off her face was in danger of pinging off like an elastic band. 'He's not that bad you know.'

'Oh yeah?' Lisa wasn't convinced. 'Look at them, four sheets to the wind and we ain't even out of the coach.' Billy had smuggled a hip flask on board and by the looks of him was well on his way, but then so were the small group who had sat at the back of the coach, smoking, singing and drinking all the way here. Thinking about it, Karen found herself understanding Lisa's point of view.

'Well, he's okay most of the time,' she replied, but even she was beginning to doubt her own words. They had been going out, if that was the right way to describe it, for about two weeks now. The truth was he went down the pub and she was allowed to go with him, he meeting his mates, she sitting there and nursing a half of bitter that lasted all night.

'You can do so much better, you know,' Lisa said, as they finally walked down the steps and stood in the bright sunshine, a salty freshness to the air from the sea.

Could she do any better? She doubted it. Even when she sat beside a lad on a coach, he paid more attention to a book than her! What chance did she have, eh? She was just happy that someone was interested in her enough to even want to go out with her. 'Really, do any better, me? Fat chance.' she shrugged in resignation.

'Yes, you can. And when you meet him, you'll know he's the one in seconds.'

Lisa and Karen had known each other since the start of school in Pitsea, and now worked together, packing cooked biscuits into boxes as they came down the flat conveyor belt. At the other end the boxes were gathered together and eventually loaded into the vans that drove them out to the shops and stores in and around Basildon, Wickford and sometimes as far afield as Brentwood. Billy worked on the supply line, getting the flat packed boxes into the hoppers that the packing girls used. That was how he had met her, walking between the lines and chatting with the girls.

Just then, Billy staggered over and threw an arm over Karen's shoulder.

'Alright, Kaza,' he said by way of a greeting, planting a moist and smoky kiss on her cheek. Karen stopped herself from pulling away because his breath was ripe with alcohol. He turned to Lisa. 'Alright, Lisa. Turned anyone to stone recently, eh?' He laughed, the lads he was with joining in. Lisa wrinkled her nose but didn't grace him with a reply. He unwrapped his arm and joined his mates. 'We're going on a pub crawl, you coming?' he said as he walked away, pointing to a pub the other side of the car park and near the entrance to the pier.

'Erm, okay,' she said hesitantly, 'I'll be over in a minute.' But he was already no longer paying any attention.

A cloud passed in front of the sun and, in typical summer fashion, from what was a perfectly clear sky, a sheet of warm rain dropped over them. Lisa shrieked with laughter as she got soaked, Karen joining in and looking for somewhere to run to get out of the surprise shower. There was a wooden bus shelter near the yellow sand of the beach and in seconds they were huddled under it.

'Where the hell did that come from?' said Lisa, as the rain bounced like marbles off the hot tarmac of the car park. 'I'm absolutely soaked.' Other people crammed under the shelter and very soon Karen found herself being pushed back into the rain. This was not how she imagined her day at the beach would be like, soaked to the skin and starting to feel cold. The rain stopped after a couple of minutes, the sun reappearing as the cloud moved on to annoy people further inland.

She started to move away from the shelter when Lisa gasped and stopped her.

'What's wrong?' Karen asked quickly, and Lisa

5

pointed. Karen looked down and was suddenly mortified. She had decided to wear a thin, white, lacy cotton blouse as it was so hot when she got up that morning. But now, in the rain and soaked through, it had turned completely transparent, clinging like a second skin to her. She threw her arms across her chest, horrified. What was she going to do? She couldn't go anywhere like this. The day was ruined.

And then she felt a large jacket being draped over her shoulders, swamping her arms and covering her front. She pulled the jacket shut around her without even thinking about where it had come from, or who owned it.

'There you go,' a voice said, 'you're safe now.'

Karen looked up and saw a smiling face with deep green eyes set beneath well groomed and short, light, hair. It was the lad she had sat beside on the coach on the way down.

'I'm Steve,' he said. He held out his hand and laughed as she tried to sneak a hand out to return the shake without opening the front of the jacket. Karen couldn't help it and laughed back. He pointed to the book in the jacket's pocket. 'Sorry, I wasn't much company on the way down. I'm taking the fireman's exam for the local fire service on Monday and was trying to get a bit of revision in.' He looked slightly embarrassed.

Karen felt her face blush. 'I'm Karen, and that's okay,' she said.

'So, erm, do you like candyfloss?' he asked awkwardly.

She nodded, suddenly lost for words.

'Well, if you want, I'll buy you some candyfloss while you dry out?'

Karen looked at Steve properly for the first time and knew what her answer would be straight away.

'Okay, thanks, that'll be great.' She suddenly remembered Lisa and looked around for her friend, but she was with her boyfriend and was walking away. Lisa looked back and just winked.

Karen smiled, knowing what she meant when she said 'in seconds' earlier.

****

The knock at the bedroom door brought Karen back to the present.

'Mum, Dad's here,' a voice called through the door. It was her eldest, Judith. Karen knew what she was going to do and, when she was ready, she went downstairs. Judith's eyebrows went up when she saw what her mum was wearing, but she said nothing, shushing everyone else into the back room, the grandchildren doing their best to be quiet. Karen joined them and Judith switched the light off.

They heard a key rattling in the lock and the door being opened, then the sound of someone walking into the hallway followed by the click of the front door being shut. Moments later, the door to the back room they were in opened and a hand reached out to turn the light on.

'Surprise!' everyone shouted, party poppers going off with lots of cheering to follow, the little voices the loudest. 'Happy birthday, Granddad,' they shouted jumping up and down in the excitement.

The man blinked in surprise, his shocked face turning into a broad smile when he saw everyone standing there.

'Blimey,' he said as he came over to Karen, green eyes glinting, hair still as fair though maybe not as thick as it once was. He placed a bag emblazoned with an Essex Fire Brigade star on the floor. 'So, this is what you were planning. I wondered why you were so tense this morning,' he said as he looked at his wife. 'And I see you found the jacket, eh?' He smiled and reached out to pull her into his arms and gave her a long kiss, oblivious to the 'ahhhs' around him. 'I found it in the loft the other day so I got it cleaned and put it with the other old suits and stuff in the wardrobe,' he whispered as he hugged her. 'I knew you'd find it when you were doing your clean out. So, going to give that one away to charity, love?' he asked.

Karen shook her head, smiling. The jacket was far, far too big for her, but it still fitted perfectly.

Oops Upside Your Head – Emma Marks ©

As I raised my arm to brush my hair, my elbow jogged against Tina's. Her mascara wand flicked a line of black across her nose.

'Oi, Careful,' she laughed, and we rearranged ourselves at her small mirror and continued to primp.

The main focus was hair I remember.

Hair had to be HUGE in 1987. We both sported permed and highlighted shoulder length blonde hair. It had been blow-dried with our heads upside down and then back combed to fluff it out still further. We scrunched in gel and then hairspray to hold it and teased it again. Once finished, the resulting hair stood out wide around our heads, in a thick, rather crunchy cloud.

We were now applying make-up, with almost comic inexperience, to our sixteen-year-old faces in order to look older. The application of lots of eyeliner took a steady hand. The dressing table was a chaos of eyeshadow, lipsticks, creams and bottles. In the middle of it all, stood a rather old, slightly sticky bottle of Martini that Tina had liberated from her parent's drinks cabinet. Two Silk Cut cigarettes burned in the ashtray, adding to the humid fug.

The bedroom was tiny, with posters of Madonna, looking impossibly perfect, on every wall. We didn't care that we were packed in like sardines – it was part of the fun to get ready together, sharing our potions, clothes and jewellery to ensure the perfect look.

We were so very excited. Our exams had just finished and we had both raised two fingers to Billericay School and walk out of its doors for the last time. In a fortnight, Tina was due to start a trainee scheme at Lloyds Bank in the High Street and I had an apprenticeship at Ford of Dagenham, lined up for September.

In our minds, we were adults now. No more school, we were going to be working, then learning to drive and making our new lives. *Definitely* not kids anymore. We wanted to be grown up.

So where to go to celebrate? We were veterans of the Billericay 'Scene' – The Canon Roche Disco, school friends' parties when their parents went out, hanging about outside off licences and in Mill Meadows in groups, looking moody and intimidating (probably).

'Tina, Emma!' the emphasised syllables underlined impatience. 'Teee-na, Emm- merr!' Tina's older sister, Marie, was yelling now from downstairs. At twenty, Marie was the very pinnacle of sophistication to us: smart, pretty and so very cool. She knew everything that mattered to a sixteen-year-old girl and I really wished she was my sister.

For some time we had pleaded with, and then later begged, Marie, to take us with her to the famed Racquel's Nightclub in Basildon where she went most Friday nights. She had seen bands such as Depeche Mode, Yazoo and Culture Club there. Members of the cast of *EastEnders* had been seen in there and reports of crazy scenes, custard wrestling and many fights added to the rumour mill of this fabled place to be.

Raquel's was out of reach to Tina and me due to it being six miles away from Billericay and that the buses stopped at 9pm. It was also out of bounds, as we were too young to get in. I grabbed my handbag and checked the loaned driving licences of Marie and her friend, Rhonda, were inside. No photo ID in 1987! We stepped carefully, like baby giraffes, down the stairs in our stiletto heels. Tina's were shocking pink and mine were silver. The Essex girl jokes of that time meant that we never wore white ones!

The glamorous and poised, Marie and Rhonda were waiting in the hallway by the front door. As we got closer, Marie looked amused.

'Have you got enough slap on?' she said. 'Look at the state of 'em, Rhond.' She plucked a bunch of tissues out of her handbag, grabbed Tina's chin and swiped at her face, wiping the surplus of blusher and foundation to a more sensible level. I submitted to the same.

'This is what happens when you put make up on in the half dark – you need to see yourselves in natural light. Now – get in the car.' She indicated mock impatience with her thumb.

We piled into the back of Marie's battered Fiesta XR2 and Tina pulled out a plastic bottle of coke which had been laced with Bacardi Rum. Marie looked into her rear-view mirror at the hiss of the top unscrewing.

'Don't you bloody spill that on my car or that skirt I lent you, Teen,' she said. 'Where did you say you were going tonight to Mum? I am for it if she finds out I took you with me.'

'I said we were going to a friend's party at their house and you were dropping us off and picking us up, like the lovely sister you are,' said Tina, giggling.

'Hmm.' Marie grimaced. 'I am still not sure this is a good idea. You need to stay in the middle of our group as we go in, don't giggle in that stupid way or say anything, until we are inside the club. Stay near us, at all times. If they don't let you in – I will have to bring you home again.'

It felt so deliciously dangerous and forbidden. Tina and I grinned and made faces, hiding our nerves. We drove past Gloucester Park Swimming Pool and I remembered the swimming gala of the previous year there, with other schools, and suddenly felt a wave of nostalgia for innocent times now behind us.

Marie turned into a side road near the town centre and then pulled up on a driveway in front of the small houses there. Two guys and three girls came out of the house – Marie's friends. The guys were wearing smart shirts with skinny ties, their hair gelled into spiked perfection. The girls wore, as we all did, bright colours, short skirts and large, chunky jewellery. I suddenly felt very young, gawky and out of place next to them.

No going back now. Tina and I linked arms and tottered along behind Marie and her friends. We followed through a subway under the main roads and into a passageway that connected the outside ring roads to the pedestrian shopping area of Basildon Town Centre. Tina and I had been shopping here on many a Saturday but it looked so different in the evening. A tall tower block of flats loomed above us and the wind whistled through the deserted shops on either side of the main street. McDonalds was still open and there were some cars going into the many multi story car parks that backed onto the shops near the cinema. We walked on and through to the bus station area where the market was during the daytime. Groups of people stood outside a full pub. Zig zagging, we joined the end of a long queue outside an unremarkable concrete building that I had never really noticed before. I could see we would wait a while. An illuminated neon sign was high on the wall, a triangle with 'Raquel's II – The Discotheque' shining out.

Eventually we reached the front, Tina and I giggled and then fell silent as we received a glare from Marie. Three large men in black leather jackets were subjecting a group of six lads in front of us to an inspection.

'You're not coming in; no trainers, no jeans.' One of the bouncers stated with finality.

Various protests came from the lads, including the fact that they had been let in the week before in trainers.

'I don't care. Are you deaf, son? You- are-not-coming-in.'

'They never let large groups of boys in,' Marie muttered to us, 'girls, yes but boys no.'

Two of the bouncers moved menacingly forwards towards the protesting lads who took involuntary steps backwards, effectively moving out of our way. The protests gave way to shouting and swearing.

The distracted, remaining doorman, cast a quick look over our group, unclipped the rope to nod us through and then joined his colleagues forming a human wall of muscle between the lads and the door.

We were in! I genuinely thought we were going to get rumbled.

Marie paid and we stood back, my initial impression was of purple – the walls and grubby carpet clashing madly as we went further up the stairs. Posters of events of yesteryear and painted shapes and murals added to the effect. The bass thump of the music was in our ears together with that club smell – a thick blend of beer, smoke, various perfumes and sweaty bodies.

The main club area was surprisingly large and looked a bit old-fashioned to my eyes. I had been expecting something very modern, glitzy and space age. A long bar in dark wood on one side, a wooden floor area, carpet on the rest, tables and chairs around the outside. It looked like (and indeed was in fact) an old ballroom and the addition of various lighting rigs and glitter balls above, with the DJ station at one end were clearly later additions.

Lots of people were there already; the room was two-thirds full with people three or four deep around the bar, getting drinks.

'It's a bit quieter in Strings, next door,' shouted Marie, over the music, 'but you wanted Raquel's, yes?'

Tina and I shrugged in unison. We didn't know really, what we wanted. We just wanted to see this strange new world.

Rhonda held out her hand. 'Right, tenner each for the whip.'

We rummaged for purses and Rhonda went to get drinks.

Marie pulled us over to a corner, with a stern expression.

'So, I will get you one alcoholic drink each, then its Coke for the rest, do NOT even attempt to buy drinks yourself – you will get us thrown out because you are underage. Don't take drinks off of anyone else and never put your drink or handbag down. Don't go into the loos alone, go together …' her voice tailed off. 'Tina, are you even listening?'

'Yes, Mum,' said Tina, earning herself a slap on her upper arm from her sister.

'I mean it, be careful. There are a lot of dodgy people here. It's good as well, but there is a lot you don't know yet in life.'

What could she possibly mean? We knew everything – we were sixteen!

The music got louder suddenly and the DJ shouted to the crowds to dance.

Marie grinned. 'OK – go dance, the DJ is great – he's been here for years, Keith – I think his name is, he's really funny sometimes.'

I Found Lovin' by The Fatback Band was playing. Tina, Marie and I, joined the floor to dance joining in with the chorus – *'whoooo-oo, I - found - love'* which everyone shouted. The music was a mixture of old and new, dance music, soul, R&B, chart music and old classic floor fillers.

It got hotter, really smoky and more crowded, as more

people came in as the pubs closed. I loved watching people, looking at what they were wearing, what they did and listening in on what they were saying but it struck me that many just stood there and they didn't look very happy or like they were enjoying themselves. We felt awkward – it was clear that when you came to this place a lot, you knew the faces there. Marie and friends were with a huge group now – we just didn't know how to interact with these older people or what they were talking about.

Tina and I were used to our crowd who, being younger, did silly things, mucked about and giggled a lot. It seemed to me that some of the people around us were trying too hard to be very "grown up" almost and that they had to be there and be seen somehow.

As people got more relaxed into the evening, it became more fun, the dancing more exuberant and people laughed, jostled and yelled to each other over the thumping beat. Then, inevitably it seemed, a fight suddenly broke out – a lad fell backwards blood gushing from his nose and down his white shirt, other lads pushed and shoved, fists flew. A girl was trying to pull a lad away, and several lads held the arms of another. Two of the bouncers from the door appeared as if by magic, jogging in that awkward way the overly-muscled have and entered the fray, which had now been surrounded by a ring of watchers. Picking up one fighting lad by his collar, the doorman dragged him to his feet and propelled him towards the exit.

'OUT!' he yelled. The lad's face was red and sweating; he was struggling to speak due to the tight grip the bouncer had on his shirt collar. We stepped back as the others passed by, on their way to being ejected. The crowd on the dancefloor filled the space left like a liquid, almost immediately and the dancing went on, to the music which had continued throughout the scene.

Almost as a response to the incident, the DJ put on a

change of tempo track. The very familiar intro to *'Oops Upside Your Head'* boomed out and in obedience to their leader, the crowd formed into several long lines, sitting on the floor, legs each side of the person in front. They rowed back and forth to the rhythm and then side to side, arms high and then slapping the floor on each side. Tina and I joined the back of one line. There must have been several hundred people all doing this strange dance – how it ever came about in the first place, is one of life's great mysteries!

We survived our first night out in the young adult world thanks to the watchful eye of Marie, who I reflected in later years, was right to be so cautious with us. We were absolutely too young to be in there but she had enough wisdom to know that we needed to find this out for ourselves, as we were so convinced at the time that we should be. We had a real experience that night, some of it fun, some of it strange and shocking. Growing older we would find it less so and know how to keep ourselves away from trouble. We would form our own groups to socialise with.

As for Raquel's – I look back with nostalgia and fondness for the place. I returned a few times, once legally old enough (with my own driving licence in my handbag!) and enjoyed the club. The "rough" reputation it had in the 1980s added to its mystique, which was of course, all mainly by word of mouth in the days before social media. Yes, you needed to be careful and yes, there were drugs and fights, but it was also a good night out and like so many reports we heard, the acts of a minority caused the whole place to be judged as if everyone that ever went to Raquel's in the 80s were dodgy. The majority of people that I knew at that time, who went there, just had some drinks, danced and had a laugh with their mates.

A Woman, a Dog, and a Dark Secret
Janet Howson ©

The first time I saw her I was cutting through the park to get to a quiz night in Northlands Park Community Centre. It was pitch black. There never had been any lights in the park and I didn't usually choose to walk between the dark skeletons of the trees waving their long branches eerily in front of me. I told myself it wasn't far and I could soon see the comforting lights of the building ahead, a beacon in the dark.

Then I made out a shape ahead but couldn't distinguish any detail except that something white was picking up the reflection of the slender moon. The shape was moving towards me. As we got closer I peered into the blackness and made out what appeared to be a female figure in a long, black coat with the hood up obscuring her face. What fascinated me though, was the figure was steering a child's pushchair and as we passed each other I could see that the white shape was a small dog sitting upright in the chair. I laughed to myself. How unusual? The figure passed me. I continued my journey and forgot about the incident.

The second time I saw her I had popped out to post a letter. I wanted to catch the early collection so I thought I'd get it into the box the evening before. The woman was walking towards me again. I noticed this time that she shuffled noiselessly, so I assumed she was wearing soft shoes. I was fascinated. Head down the figure was moving at quite a pace and we were soon passing each other. I tried to gain eye contact. The head however was down and the hood again obscured my vision. I could see the flimsy hemline of a flowered dress hanging below the bottom of her coat. The dog was still sitting up in the pram, silent, watching. I turned to look behind me to see where she had gone but she must have turned down one of the avenues as she was nowhere to be seen. I shrugged and continued towards the post box.

The third time I saw her I was determined to make her look at me. I wanted to know why this stranger was walking the streets with a dog in a pram at night. How old was she? Where did she live?

I was coming home from a meeting at the Bas Centre. She was walking at her fast shuffling pace, again. Her feet were obviously troubling her. The white dog was in the same position, glued to the seat, no barking, no panting, just silence. Perhaps I could stroke the dog. That would be a good way to find out who she was. Pleased with the idea I carried on until we were adjacent.

'Good evening, it's certainly a chilly one. What is your dog called?' That was all I managed to get out as she shuffled quickly past me, hood up, head down. I was tempted to follow her but then she might think I was stalking her and be frightened, so I left it and continued on home.

Was I getting obsessed with this woman and her dog? It was if she was haunting me. Perhaps I ought to ignore them both. Forget about them. Yet there was something compelling about her. I felt there was more to her than just a lonely woman walking her dog in the cover of night. Almost as if she was trying to show me something by the fact she kept on passing me in the dark. She could cross the road but never did.

The next time I saw her I was determined to keep up my resolve and ignore her. I could take another route home which would mean I would be walking in the same direction as her so I would not meet her face to face. Satisfied with my plan I waited for my next evening event. It was after the Basildon Book Club meeting. We usually finished about 10.30pm and luckily it would mean I was walking down the same road she always walked but I would be behind or in front of her. I was in a good mood after a couple of glasses of wine and a productive discussion on the book choice. I was thinking about my evening and I couldn't see any shuffling figure.

Then she was there. She seemed to appear out of nowhere. She was standing right in front of me, only the dog in the pram divided us. It gave me a shock. For the first time I felt uneasy. What was she trying to tell me? I opened my mouth to speak but I didn't know what to say. Then, before I had gathered my thoughts she had shuffled past me and disappeared around the next corner. I stood for a few minutes gathering my thoughts. Then I carried on my way home determined to find something out about her.

Later that week I was passing a group of dog walkers in Northlands Park. They always seemed to be there, chatting more than exercising their canine companions. I had an idea and approached them.

'Hi, I wondered if any of you know a woman who wears a long black coat with a hood and has a white dog in a pushchair?'

The three of them looked at each other quizzically. 'Sorry, never seen anyone like that. What about you, Myra? You're here more than me.'

'No, I think I'd remember her if she had a dog in a pushchair. You don't know her name then?'

'No, I've tried to talk to her but she's always in a hurry. She tends to be out at night on her own, except for the dog. I think she's quite elderly.'

'I know who might know her,' the third dog owner chipped in, 'Brian, he is here every day. Sits on the bench he bought after his wife died. He had a plaque put on it with her name and her date of birth and death. Sad really, I don't think he's ever got over it.' She turned round, pointing towards a lone figure on a bench at the end of the footpath, looking over the football field. 'Go and ask him.'

'Thank you, I'll do just that. Enjoy the rest of your day.' I left them and strode towards the sitting figure. He looked round when I got closer. He was probably in his eighties.

'Good morning, could I join you?'

He studied my face, 'As long as you are not selling anything or talking loudly on your mobile phone.'

'No.' I sat down on the bench. 'I just wanted to ask you if you knew an elderly lady who walks her white dog in a pushchair?'

He stared hard at me, then pointed to the plaque on the back of the seat. 'See that? That is in memory of my dear wife. This was her favourite place. I can sit here and remember her.' He paused. 'We had a white Highland Terrier. She loved that dog. Probably more than she loved me.' He paused and smiled ruefully. 'Poor thing became crippled with arthritis so she came up with the idea of pushing him about in a pushchair. Everyone used to chuckle when they saw her, but she didn't care. Never took any notice of what other people thought as long as the dog was happy. She would have died for that dog.' He paused, looking out onto the field where a group of young boys were kicking a football about. 'I lost them both together.' He turned to look at the plaque. 'I was with them at the end.' He laughed. 'It will have been the two of them you saw.'

I felt a chill down my spine and found it difficult to take in what he was saying. Was he actually implying I had seen a ghost? I didn't believe in ghosts but the man didn't seem at all surprised I'd seen her. It was as if she was still alive. I really didn't know what to say. I drew a deep breath and tried to appear calm as if it was the most natural thing in the world to have seen his dead wife.

'Oh, you must miss her terribly and the dog too. What were their names?' I could hear him chatting on but it was a haze of words. At the soonest possible moment I found an excuse to go and crossed the park to return home. I repeated to myself that I didn't believe in ghosts. There must be a logical explanation.

The last time I saw her, I came across her suddenly as I turned a corner. I was returning from a friend's house in a road opposite the park. It was very late for me and my friend had lent me a torch. As she shuffled towards me I shone my torch at her and noticed there was a difference. There were two patches of white: the dog and something else. Strangely I didn't feel frightened.

Then I made out what it was. The hood was down and my torch picked up the white shape. It was her skull, the jaw open in a scream. A scream of pain. I felt the breath leave my body, the shock paralysing. Then I noticed the dog. My stomach heaved. Its white coat was stained with blood, the eyes terrified. It was if they were trying to tell me something. Something about the way they died. Who had done this to an elderly lady and an innocent dog?

Then I remembered his words and the look on his face.

'I was with them at the end.'

I knew I would never see her again. I now knew what she had wanted to tell me. A dark, sinister secret that meant she could never rest until she could pass it on to someone else. She had chosen me. It was up to me now as to what I would do with it.

The Translator Unit's on the Fritz
Saul Ben ©

Freaking stasis chamber stinks like monkey took a ⇦▶↘▲ in it – yeah, once a day for at least a thousand years. I gag, but my ▽◀↕↘⇨△⇨↑→▽ empty, been off solids for the last freak knows how long. Tugging the nutrient tubes from my throat, more gagging. One foot out of the chamber, testing the ground. And, of course, testing my strength. ∧↑⇨ ⇨←←↕△◀ ↓▽ ⇨◣↑⇨▶▽◀↓↔→↘ My muscle mass has turned to jelly, despite the auto-stimulation, and my bones feel like sticks of chalk. I give it ⇨ ⇨↕▶▲↙⇨ of goes, and eventually I manage to crawl out. Panting, I struggle to stand, one foot after the other, I think ◀↑⇨◀→▽ how it goes. First order ↕← ◀↑⇨ ⇦⇨◢ is a physical work-up, after that hydration, nutrition, hygiene, in that order, then ↘⇨◢⇦⇨ a long crawl to the gym, get some of my strength back. The life support is humming, there's another chamber open. I check the name plate on the lid. Oh, her. The rest of the ⇨↑⇨↘⇦⇨△▽ are still occupied. All functioning bar two, I just can't bring myself to check the ↔⇨↘⇨▽ of the deceased. So, I shuffle to the scanner. A bright red laser runs over my naked and emaciated form. Yuk. (Clothes, ◀↑⇨◀→▽ something else to put on the things to do list.) My medical diagnostics just about check out, so that means ↘◢ internal organs are still functional, albeit borderline. ↻⇨⇨↙↙◢ doesn't feel like it though. But limbs all there, I'd lost a finger and a couple of toes, ⇦▶◀ give it a few weeks and they'll grow back though. Sex organs intact, ←⇨△ ⇨▽ ⇶ can see, so all's good, right? Okay, so guys, you can probably tell the freaking translator unit's on the fritz, ▲△↕⇦⇨↙◢ like everything else on this tin can. That amount of time passes, what d'you expect? Hopefully most of this message is still readable, otherwise I'm talking to myself. Not that that's not a pleasure, of course. Okay so, plan is, get myself reorientated and wake up the chief engineer, gonna be ⇨ busy old boy. ⁀↕↧ I'm working on the basis ◀↑⇨◀ as my cryo chamber was sprung we ⇨△⇨ approaching our destination. ↺↙⇨⇨▽⇨ don't tell me it's a false alarm. I check the temporal readout, wow. I whiz round the dial (↔↕ shame in analogue) atomic time, celestial time, galactic time and select local units. Four thousand (of your Earth, tee hee) years since departure ←△↕↘ our system, that's, ◀↑⇨◀→▽, wow. ⇶ look around the old tub at the corroding metalwork, ◀↑⇨ accumulation of, of, what the hell is that ▽◀▶←←. Hey, I say out loud, d'ya think the warranty's run out ◢⇨◀↰' Okay, so it wasn't so funny. But that's the first time I'd heard my voice in↘↘↘ Feels like I went to sleep only just yesterday. Correction. It feels like I went to sleep only just yesterday... following a three week drinking binge, a tumble down an infinitely long flight of concrete steps, having fought off the attentions of an amorous →△⇨↘⇨↙↓⇨↔, been chased by its pet arthropod, taken refuge in a cave which turned out to be the gaping mouth of a giant sabre-toothed ▷↕↙▽◀↕△⇨↗ and, having passed through its alimentary canal ⇨↔⇦ just managed to dig my way out of a pile steaming dung only to discover it's raining warm vomit, and my bones have just turned into freaking chewing gum. Again, not so funny, but deep space, it does weird things to your head. Radiation's the big problem, last insult ◀↕ my sanity was the Van Allen Belt, screw that for a game of intergalactic warriors. ↳⇦⇦⇨⇦ benefit, seems to have given me ⇨ hellova suntan, that's for damned sure. Anyway, ◢↕▶ catching all this? Any problems, ↙↓↗⇨ if your device goes ⇦↙↕↕▲ every so often like mine, just slap your viewer upside the head, works at this end, might work for you, alternatively you could always call ←↕△ an engineer. If, that is, you're prepared to put up with ⇨↙↙ those supercilious geeky in-crowd smirks. Turn it off and on again. You anything like me, engineer gets one upside the head too. ↻↓→↑◀↧ so quick catch-up. Worst case, we don't make it. Yeah, boo bloody hoo (state of this craft ◀↑⇨◀→▽ more than a distinct possibility), and you pull this recording out of a pile of radioactive wreckage, best I tell you the reason we're here, right, first contact, ◢↕▶   know what I mean. Here's how ▷⇨ located you. Your Voyager One probe was passing within 1.6 light-years' ↕← the star Gliese 445 which ↖▶▽◀ happens to support our solar system, that's ↓↔ the constellation Camelopardalis, right, that being ↗↓↔⇦⇨ our back yard. ⌢↕ good shot guys. Pretty much bang on target, Nice friendly message by the way, you sound like good folks. Your probe had been travelling about 40,000 of your years when ↕▶△ sensors picked it up. What with bouncing off ◀↑⇨ occasional asteroid, smashing into ⇦◢ tens of thousands of micro-meteors, ⇨↔⇦ scoured to ⇦▶→→⇨△◢ by space dust ↓◀ wasn't exactly in showroom condition when ↓◀ reached us. ⇉↔ fact it was battered to freak knows what. ⇉← ◢↕▶ get my drift. And that pair of gold recording discs (LPs, whatever), for ▷↑↓⇨↑ thanks by the way, very informative, can't wait to meet Carl Sagen, ⇦▶◀ they were in a bit of a state, practically unplayable. ˌ⇨→◁⇨ got them mounted on the bulkhead in

the crew's rec room, all the good they were. Scratched to
↩▶→→↪△◢. So it was damned lucky we even found your
solar system, let alone your planet. Triumph of astro
navigation, yeah. Anyway, △↓→↑◀ 40,000 years had passed,
figured with your primitive technology you'd ⇨↙↙ be
extinct, know what I mean. ⌒↕ rather than miss you, our
science guys tweaked the space/time continuum, and
hopefully you'll still be around ↩↕▷↔　◀↑↪△↪. Deliver
a bit of a warning. You know, we don't want to turn up and
you're out, you know ▷↑↪◀ I mean. Like we open the hatch
and it's the freaking Mesozoic, and some dirty great lizard's
▷↪↓◀↓↔→ for his lunch. So we performed a bioscan.
You know what a bioscan is right? Health check for your
planet. Results came back: dangerously depleted ozone
layer, mass extinctions, rainforests burning, rampant
desertification, background radiation ↪◀ an all time high,
ice caps melting, atmosphere toxic with pollution. ⌒↕ we
figured, yes mankind's around all right, twenty-first century
if ⇉→↘ not mistaken, based on pollution levels. We've
arrived just in time, fifty years later and we'd have missed
you, along with the dinosaurs. So red warning, right, cease
and desist – industrialisation, consumerism, fosil fuels, time to
stop. Or don't, and give the cockroaches their turn.
↳↔◢▷↪◢↕ our voyage supervisor Jessica was reactivated
couple of hours before me. Said something typically insulting,
like she couldn't trust the crew to keep their hands to
themselves when she was deep in cryogenesis so she set the
alarm early. Freaking cheek, as if... ⌒↪↓↩ I like em young,
anything over 4,000 years is a bit too mature for my taste. ⌒↕
anyway, ◀↑↪ external sensors are busted, we're flying blind,
approaching ↪↔ unfamiliar planet. VS Jessica looks at me,
like wooo. So suit up, she says, and I find myself press-ganged
to hull inspection duty. Out ◀↑↪ hatch I pop. ↳↔↩ what a
state we're in, burn marks ↪↙↙ down one side, nose cone
melted, guidance system shot away, meteor strikes ▶▲ and

down the hull, ⇨↔⇦ we've got half-a-dozen weather satellites in tow, caught up on what's left ⇕← our solar sail, dragging a mile and a half behind us. ↳↔⇦ that's really not very good at all. So ⇉ report back. ∧↑⇨ unit's cattled, I say. Beyond repair. Jessica goes into ⇨ right strop. Without a guidance system, how the hell ⇨△⇨ we gonna locate ⇕▶△ landing zone. Where ◀↑⇨ hell is Washington DC anyway? ⇉ catch a look in Jessica's eye. ⇉◀→▽ not just me that's holding back the panic. ⌒⇕ we get to rousting out the rest ⇕← the crew. Think of it, six crew members emerging from cryo chambers at once, that's 4,000 years ⇕← accumulated body odour. They stink like deep space polecats, ya know what I mean? ▽⇕ before we do anything →⇨◀ ◀⇕ hosing them down, passing out ◀↑⇨ roll-on. When they're sanitised, dressed and fed ⇨↔⇦ less malodorous we assemble them ↓↔ the briefing room. This is the situation, know what I ↘⇨⇨↔. Navigation officer says nothing else for it, have to steer the bastard manually. I'm thinking, brace for impact. Two thirds of ◀↑⇨ place is water, ↑⇨ ▽⇨◢▽, we might get lucky ⇨↔⇦ hit something squidgy. ∧↑⇨↔ he has his assistant, that's cute little Nerris Jones, check ↑↓▽ charts. She reports, ←△⇕↘ what she can tell, the whole nav system is totally fried. We'll be lucky we don't overshoot the planet, let alone score any part of the USA. Jessica opens ◀↑⇨ viewing port. ↵⇨ all rush to have a gander. ↳↔⇦ it's there, that blue green beauty. ↵⇨→△⇨ just going to have to eyeball it, says the sleepy navigator, taking his seat at t↑⇨ nav consol. Me I'm thinking ↓◀→▽ time to kiss my ⇨▽▽ goodbye. Miracle of miracles the nav screen momentarily flickers to life. ↵⇨ all gather round, landing coordinates begin to appear. ⇥▶◀ landing coordinates for where? Attended a course on terrestrial geography before we left ⇨↔⇦ I don't recognise the place. ↳↔⇦ we're thinking, well it ain't DC, ⇦▶◀ any port right? Let's just hope ◀↑⇨ natives are friendly. ⌒⇕ we come in hot. Skimming ⇨↔⇦ skipping through the atmosphere, ↳↔⇐ we start picking up place names on the nav consol – Qu⇨bec Winn↓peg, Vanc⇕uver, To↗yo, Beijin→, Kabu↙, Mosc⇕w, Cope↔hagen, Great W⇨kering, Eastwo⇕d, Thund⇨rsley, Pit▽ea, and suddenly... There's ◀↑⇨ unmistakable sound of an intergalactic homing beacon. What the very freak? Below us there's habitation, ⇨↔⇐ we're tumbling now, ⇕↔↙▲ barely in control. ∧↑⇨ ground's coming up fast. The navigator struggles to avoid areas of population. ↳◀ the last minute he attempted to divert to wide stretch of river. But ◀⇕ no effect, ◀↑⇨ beacon's coordinates seemed locked firmly in. We hit hard, bouncing, then we're in water, skipping over a lake like a pebble. And finally we come to rest. Floating, bobbing ▶▲ and down, glowing red ↓↔ a cloud of steam. Jessica opens ◀↑⇨ view port. There's a sign ⇕↔ the far bank. Northlands Fishing Lake. There's a clang on the hull. ⇉ open the hatch. Two guys in ⇨ rowing boat. Hi-vis jackets.

'Did you book this slot?' One of them yells: 'Only we've got two more coming in tonight.'

***

An unidentified object sped through the sky at 2,000 mph over Basildon ... one of the unexplained sightings reported to Essex Police in the past five years. Details of the Unidentified Flying Objects (UFOs) seen over the county have been revealed in a freedom of information request from the Local Democracy Reporting Service. It shows that there were 37 sightings reported to Essex Police between 2014 and 2019 and Basildon made up almost 30 per cent with 11 sightings. One witness in Wickford phoned the police this year to report what they said, 'looked like two drones on fire'. The objects caused "really fast streams of light similar to a flare" and the caller described the sighting to the police as 'out of this world'.

In another report from 2016, a Basildon caller described seeing three 'craft'. One was seen flying into the sky at speeds of 'about 2,000mph' while the remaining two 'disappeared'. Police received five reports from Southend over the same period, with all but one spotted in Westcliff.

The last paragraph was reproduced with kind permission of the THURROCK AND SOUTH ESSEX INDEPENDENT

Proof and Experiment – Liz Keeble ©

Sue Jones ran a protective hand over her burgeoning seven-month-old bump. It was Christmas Eve 1968 and she was shopping for last minute bits and pieces that would make her and Tony's last Christmas as "just the two of them" absolutely perfect. They were expecting in the spring and things were just as they should have been for every newly married couple and their honeymoon pregnancy. Two glorious weeks on the Cornish coast the previous August had seen to it that Sue was well and truly with child on their return – a bit sooner than they had anticipated – but as a devout Roman Catholic couple, their contraceptive practices were – not to put too fine a point on it – grossly inadequate but baby Jones was very welcome and the young couple couldn't wait to meet their new arrival. Tony had spent much of his Christmas break decorating the nursery – lemon and white – and Sue was going through her nest building phase and had planned Christmas down to the last cocktail cherry. She was taking an eleventh hour trip to the local shops to pick up a couple of items she'd forgotten. Not that she couldn't manage without a back-up supply of Oxo cubes or Ovaltine – did her cravings extend to items beginning with "O?" It just seemed prudent to make sure they were in the house. Just in case.

It was cold and it was miserable. The leaden skies had persisted for days and the sinister mist rolling in at their end of the Thames Estuary was making the Christmas season feel positively Dickensian. Sue never really gave the weather a second thought. Both she and Tony came from military families where there was no such thing as bad weather, only bad clothing. But today? Today, as she shuffled along the high street, the mist, those clouds, that icy chill brought with them a sense of impending doom. As this inexplicable fear tightened its bony frigid fingers around her throat, Sue cradled her bump, almost wrapping herself around it to reinforce its defences. God forbid anything should happen to this tiny unborn human whose fingers and toes she had yet to count. Sue shuddered at the unthinkable and stepped up her pace towards home. By the time she put the key in the front door, thoughts of chestnut stuffing, bread sauce and the challenge of keeping nine different vegetables warm crowded her fleetingly troubled mind and the sense of impending doom dissipated like the mist that had ushered it in.

Within twenty-four hours, Christmas had been and gone. It had been a blast with the Party Sevens, snowballs and Babychams and there were plenty of polaroids to show the grandchildren. Before they knew it, it was New Year's Eve and they were on their way in the freezing cold to Tony's friend Paul's where they and the other five couples from the wild-fowling crowd always spent a rowdy and hilarious New Year. There were the inevitable drinking games and conversations about the arrival of baby Jones, the first among the group of friends. The men were hoping it would be a boy and that he would become a seasoned wild-fowler with their expert coaching; the women were unsurprisingly horrified by this aspiration: the thought of a small child being taught how to use a gun! They wanted a little girl that they could buy pretty clothes for and parade around the park in the impressive Silver Cross coach-built pram that Sue's parents had bought for their first grandchild. It was a great night. Memorable. Full of laughs.

When Sue and Tony left at about 1am, there was already a thick frost. The windows of the parked cars were opaque but the sky was clear and bright. 'See you on Saturday afternoon,' called Tony. 'You bet!' replied Paul. 'I'll pick you up about 2.30?' In the midst of the New Year celebrations, the men folk had managed – somehow – to organise a wild-fowling expedition for the following Saturday at Maplin Sands. 'Love it out there!' Bob had enthused. 'Miles and miles of empty shoreline and no people.' The men sighed a collective sigh, thinking of how much they would enjoy the bleak desolate seascape that had provided them with so many hours of tranquility and calm over the years.

Tony spent the next couple of days making sure his kit was clean and safe. The last thing they needed was a gun misfiring, especially out on the sands where it was difficult for the emergency services to access. They always took a military spec first aid kit – just in case – but the five Ps had been ingrained in his mind over years by his father: 'Proper preparation prevents poor performance,' he always used to say. So before an expedition Tony had always gone through the safety protocols with all his guns, all his ammo, knives etc and made sure that his kit was as thoroughly prepped and properly packed as it possibly could be: there would always be some unforeseen circumstance that might arise but he and his mates knew the sands like the back of their hand and had done similar trips dozens of times. It was all good. 'Don't suppose you've got any Oxo cubes?' he asked Sue. 'They're always handy for a hot drink on a trip.' Sue chuckled to herself as she opened the cupboard. 'Just in case … '

Saturday came and Tony closed the front door behind him, having kissed Sue and the bump goodbye and left her listening to Pete Brady on Radio 1. They couldn't afford a telly yet, especially having had to fork out on all the baby stuff, but Sue loved nothing more than sitting doing the ironing with the wireless blaring. He did question the wisdom of leaving her alone in the house with the likes of Dave Lee Travis. He still wasn't sure about Radio 1. Seemed a bit racy for his liking. He preferred Radio 2 and would rather be listening to the Frank Chacksfield Hour on a Saturday afternoon. Still. He wouldn't be there. He would be braving the elements on the hunt for geese and ducks on Maplin Sands.

Maplin Sands is a remote coastal area at the edge of South East Essex consisting of mudflats as far as the eye can see just off Foulness Island. The location and geographical features made it the ideal choice for a Ministry of Defence testing site, since the flat tidal sands provide a large safety area for long range firing and shell recovery. The British School of Gunnery opened there in 1848 and Foulness Island itself was purchased by the MOD during the First World War. The site covers over 9,300 acres with another 35,000 acres when the tide goes out… When the tide goes out at Foulness, it goes out a long way, revealing shires of sand packed hard enough to support the weight of a walker. When the tide comes back in, it comes in fast – galloping over the sands quicker than a human can run.

Tony piled his gear into the boot of Paul's car and climbed in the back seat. Don was already in the passenger seat up front.

'Alright, fellas?' he said, excited.

'Can't wait,' said Don, 'although it's a bit misty already.'

A conversation ensued about how the weather had been a little strange with some very clear overnight skies followed by dense mists.

'Please God it won't get any thicker,' said Paul peering out of the windscreen while he fiddled with the tuner. Within seconds, Pete Brady had joined them on their journey. It made Tony think of Sue cosied up indoors.

'Have we got a full complement today?' he asked.

'We do indeed!' replied Don, explaining that Steve, Bob and Richard had already set off with Steve driving and were going to meet them at Wakering Stairs, the nominated rendezvous point.

The roads were fairly deserted and it wasn't long before they were driving past the MOD police post at the entrance to the high security area of the Proof and Experimental Establishment at Foulness. They waved as they passed through as the chap on duty was well-known to them from previous visits.

'It never fails to amaze me that they just let folk through without permits or identity or anything!' exclaimed Paul. 'I mean they can't be doing anything major over here surely with security as lax as that?'

'Don't knock it!' laughed Don. 'It means we can come out here more or less as and when we please without having to battle red tape. And in any case the Broomway is a public footpath.'

The car fell silent at the mention of the Broomway. It was the path they always took to the best hunting grounds. It was indeed as Don described a public footpath whose route was stitched into any map of the area and so-called because safe passage used to be marked out with four hundred or so brooms placed between thirty and sixty yards either side of the track. But it was also known as the deadliest path in Britain and it was only on maps that its course was indelibly marked and there was a reason the four hundred brooms were there. The relentless tide, a most powerful arm of nature's artillery, the unhalting tide which came in and out twice a day every day without fail did unrelentingly wash clean away every last trace of the track itself leaving it nigh on impossible for travellers to find their way back. And once the impenetrable mist had fallen, it was unlikely that anyone would find their way their way to anywhere other than the quicksand or out to the open sea.

They arrived at Wakering Stairs and Paul pulled up noisily beside Steve's car. The small group of well-prepared, appropriately clothed and seasoned wildfowlers gathered their gear and started out through the mist across the Broomway. The men laughed, cracked jokes, fired their guns and all the while the mist hung low over the sands and the temperature dropped. After a couple of hours, Steve had had enough. The light was fading and they had not had much success in any case. The cold was eating into his bones and he made a note to reinvest in a better-insulated jacket for the next trip. He made his way back to his car, followed less than an hour later by Don and Bob. The three men sat drinking hot tea from a flask, evaluating the afternoon's excursion and catching the end of Melody Fair, with Peter Latham and his musical mixture for a winter afternoon. Country Meets Folk then came on which none of them really liked, but which was preferable to any of the other stations that they could tune into out there.

By 6pm it was pitch black and there was no sign of Tony, Paul and Richard. The three friends were now seriously concerned for the men's safety and went back out to the sands, firing their guns and shouting out in an attempt to guide them back to the agreed meeting place. By 6.30, it became apparent that their attempts were in vain, panic was setting in and so they drove back to the police post and reported the matter. The chaos that followed was to become a matter of public record. On advice from the Establishment on-duty officer, they returned to Wakering Stairs and pointed their headlights out to sea. A local man who had been in the area also joined them and drove out about three hundred yards shining his headlights in different directions. The hearts of the men became increasingly as leaden as the skies and eventually, after several abortive attempts at a search, at almost 10pm that night, the coastguard was alerted…

'They should have been back by 7.' Sue was beside herself alone in the house. She had long since silenced the radio, finished the ironing and got ready for bed. She phoned each of the wives in turn for news or updates. She made mugs of tea she never drank and burned toast that went cold while the butter remained unspread on the blade of the knife. The silence from without, shrouded by an oppressive darkness, was more deafening than the silence from within. That familiar grip of fear constricted her throat and she felt the walls of their cosy little cottage closing in around her. The rising terror made it impossible for her to keep still. She called her parents who arrived to keep her company around half past nine.

It was almost midnight when they saw the reflection of the blue lights in the front room window where they had been having a necessary cup of Ovaltine. Sue rushed to open the front door and stood paralysed, clutching her belly with one hand and her dad's arm with the other, as the two policemen emerged in what felt like slow motion from the squad car, unlocked the front gate and walked towards her. 'Mrs Anthony Jones?'

Sue gave birth to a healthy baby girl at the end of February 1969 and named her Antonia. Paul Grayson's body was washed up in a nearby creek a few weeks after that and the body of Richard Slatford was located further up the Estuary the following June. Tony's body was never found. A public enquiry into the poor handling of the situation that contributed to the men's disappearance was never held even though the matter was brought before the House of Commons twelve months later by the local MP. When the surviving friends would talk about it years later they were often perplexed as to why the only thing they could really remember from that night was what they were listening to in the car on Radio 2.

The above story is based on true events. The characters' names have been changed and the interactions between them are purely fictitious. One of the wives however was pregnant with her first child and her husband's body was never recovered.

Where the text is shown in italics, those sections are paraphrased from the following accounts:
https://api.parliament.uk/historic-hansard/commons/1970/feb/13/maplin-sands-deaths.
https://www.qinetiq.com/shoeburyness/About and http://www.bbc.com/travel/story/20170110-why-the-broomway-is-the-most-dangerous-path-in-britain

To Be a Munitionette – Dawn Knox ©

'Over my dead body!'

'But Ma!'

'You're too young, Clara!'

'I'm seventeen! I want to do my bit!'

'That's as may be, but this family has done more than its fair share for the war effort. Do I need to remind you, two of your brothers are in the trenches in France and a third is God knows where? Isn't that enough? Do I have to lose my daughter as well?'

We glared at each other.

I decided on a gentler and more reasonable approach.

'You're not going to lose me, Ma. Lots of people work in the factory. Dorothy said there are all sorts of precautions. It's important work and I want to be part of it. The ammunition they make goes to our boys at the Front. It keeps them safe.'

'Safe? Our boys are anything but safe! And you won't be either! People were blown to bits in an explosion in that factory not long ago. It was so bad it blew out windows in Vange, Pitsea and Laindon! You need your head read, my girl! And you need to stop listening to everything Dorothy tells you! Anyway, what's wrong with the job you've got? I know it's not well paid but you're not likely to get blown up scrubbing floors!'

She stopped abruptly, as if shocked by her anger. Sinking into the armchair, her eyes sought the photo of Dad on the mantelpiece and tears began to slide down her cheeks.

I'd expected resistance when I told Ma I'd got a job in the Pitsea Explosives Factory but I hadn't been prepared for such rage. We'd all relied on Ma's strength when Dad died three years ago, but now that Jimmy and Wilf are fighting in the trenches and Jack's missing in action, she's retreated into a world where fears are denied, and hopes suspended. And now, because of me, her carefully controlled emotions had exploded.

But the whole world is at war – and I want to feel I'm doing my bit for our fighting men – for my brothers.

Anyway, I've already handed in my notice at Pitsea Hall, so there's no going back. Money's been tight since Dad passed away, and as a munitionette, I'll earn 4d an hour – much more than I could, as a maid. I'll be helping the war effort and supporting our family. How can that be wrong?

But it looked like Ma might not see it that way.

When my first shift finished, Dorothy and I cycled home through the country lanes, although we were both uncharacteristically quiet.

'Will I see you tomorrow, Clara?'

'Yes.'

'I wondered … You know … what with the alarm going off today and that …'

'I'll be there.' I sounded more positive than I felt.

Waiting on the corner of her road, I watched as she cycled to her parents' bungalow. The air was tinged with the scent of freshly cut grass and I breathed deeply, filling my lungs and replacing the noxious gas that had surrounded me all day.

Gradually, my headache subsided and my churning stomach calmed. Did I really want to work in a place that made me feel so ill? Some of the girls had bright yellow skin from contact with the chemicals they worked with, yet they turned up day after day, and everyone in the factory seemed to suffer from headaches and rashes. Dorothy had laughed when I voiced my concerns, saying it was all part of the job.

I should have cycled the rest of the way home, but instead, I wheeled my bicycle slowly back to Laindon. I wanted time to reflect on the day.

It had been a long one – that was for sure. I wasn't used to working a twelve-hour shift but Dorothy had said I'd get used to it. It seemed there were many things I'd have to get used to if I wanted to be a munitionette.

But for all Dorothy's bravado, I'd seen her flinch that morning when someone had sneezed. She'd laughed once she'd realised what had caused the sudden strident sound, but the look of panic had been unmistakeable and she'd reached for the name tag she wore on a cord round her neck. In the case of explosion, the name tags we wore would be the only way of identifying what was left of a body – if indeed anything was left at all – and some of the girls seemed to treat them like lucky charms.

Of course, safety was a priority, and precautions began at the gate where everyone entering and leaving was searched. Anything that could cause a flame or spark was confiscated, such as matches, cigarettes or even metal hairpins. The uniforms we had to wear were also designed with safety in mind. There were no turn-ups on the trousers, or pockets in the overalls, so we couldn't carry anything that might start a fire. The uniforms were colour-coded, so we could only access areas where we were authorised to work, and if there was an emergency, a head-count could be carried out quickly. Long hair had to be plaited and tucked into a mob cap to avoid the risk of it getting caught in machines, and even the walkways were made of wood so that stones couldn't be picked up in our shoes and make a spark. But despite all those precautions, it would only take someone to spill or drop something, to cause a huge explosion.

During the morning I'd admired the munitionettes' relaxed attitude to their dangerous work, and wondered how long it would take me to achieve such calmness. But shortly after we'd been to lunch in the mess room, an alarm sounded and we were instructed to vacate the factory. I'd assumed it was yet another part of the daily routine – until I saw Dorothy's expression. Panic was registering on the other munitionettes' faces too as we filed out and followed the guards to a wooded area some distance away.

'The wardens at Southend, telephoned to say there's a Zeppelin raid,' someone whispered.

We huddled together in silence, listening to the eerie throbbing of the approaching German airship, and there was a collective gasp as it appeared over the horizon. I'd seen photographs of a Zeppelin in the newspaper, when one of them had dropped more than a hundred bombs on Southend-on-Sea. But nothing had prepared me for the enormous monster that pushed its way through the air, casting a gigantic, black shadow on the land.

As it came closer, I knew my legs were no longer capable of movement. But it didn't matter because there was no point running. There was no hiding place from such a huge, flying, bombing machine.

'It's in trouble ...' someone whispered as the engines faltered and died. I held my breath and prayed. For several seconds, the disabled Zeppelin hung motionless in the air until the wind caught it and slowly carried it away, back towards the coast. When it finally disappeared over the horizon, we hugged each other, hurled insults at the Germans and cheered wildly.

The soldiers led us back into the factory and we resumed

our work assembling and packing cartridges, but we no longer sang as we had during the morning. Now, everyone worked silently, listening for an alarm that would warn us the Zeppelin was coming back to blow us to bits.

And even now, hours later, the feeling of foreboding hadn't left me. As I wheeled my bicycle home, the sinking sun slipped behind a cloud and I shivered – not because of the decrease in temperature – but because it reminded me of the airship relentlessly bearing down on us.

I wondered if Ma, alone at home, had seen it, knowing that in all probability, it intended to drop bombs on the explosives factory. I had a sudden urge to get home, and climbing on my bicycle, I pedalled furiously.

When I arrived at our cottage, Ma was sobbing. Her eyes were red and swollen and I could tell she'd been crying for some time, but when she saw me, her eyes lit up.

'Clara!'

'It's all right, Ma, I'm home safe. The Zeppelin was blown away …'

How could I have been so selfish?

Hadn't Ma got enough to worry about?

I'd hand in my notice tomorrow. Nothing was worth this. And it's not as if I'd enjoyed myself. I'd had a really dreadful day.

And then I saw the letter she was holding out.

'He's coming home,' Ma whispered, 'Jack's wounded. He's in a field hospital in France, but he's safe and he's coming home …'

We clung to each other, laughing and crying, and I was filled with renewed optimism and determination.

Tomorrow, I'd return to the factory and I'd endure Zeppelin raids, headaches, rashes, bright yellow skin – whatever it took. I'd do my bit until this terrible war was over and my brothers were home once more – with Ma and me.

The Basildon Writers' Club – Wendy Ogilvie ©

The Basildon Clubs Awards ceremony seemed to drag on forever and Clay, the chairman of the Basildon Writers' Club, was more than miffed they hadn't at least got a mention for their efforts this year. Apparently, the mayor told him the idea of one word stories as the future of writing was something of an oxymoron. That, or he called Clay a poxy moron, he wasn't entirely sure as his hearing aid had been playing up.

'Bloody Knit and Natter lot,' he said shaking his head and slamming his folder onto the table. 'How hard can it be to weave a few bits of wool into something nobody wants to see whilst discussing the latest episode of *Coronation Street*?'

Darlene, the group's budding crime writer, shook her head. 'Well someone must have thought providing winter wear for inanimate objects in the town was a good thing to do because they won didn't they? I mean, why it's necessary for a lamppost to don a 20ft scarf is beyond me.'

'I agree. What a naff idea … ' said Stefan, ' … knitting winter woollies for post boxes. What they gonna do next year, swimming trunks for that naked statue in the town centre?'

They looked up as Mandy, a thirty-something council

worker, stormed into the meeting room.

'Can you Adam and Eve it? Knit and Natter winning with winter apparel? They aren't even creative. My ten-year-old neice has knitted a scarf before. They could have knitted something different, like a sofa or something. At least our idea was creative and interesting. We didn't sit here for all of five minutes and declare *'I know, let's knit stuff for the town to wear'.*'

'Perhaps someone did suggest that … ' said Stefan, ' … but actually meant for the people of the town. Like people who needed warm clothing but that Florrie who runs it took it literally and the rest were too scared to correct her.'

'You're probably right,' Clay said nodding his head, 'Florrie is a bit scary. Anyway let's move on and get this meeting underway. Now, we have to decide if we are going to go ahead with our idea for the next competition; let's have a vote shall we?'

'Better wait for Frank, you know he'll want to have his say,' said Darlene.

'Well he'd better hurry. When I say we will commence at 7pm I expect people to get here at that time.'

'Oh, stop banging your gavel judge, it's only five past,' Darlene said whilst trying to look along the corridor. 'Here he comes now.'

Frank, a retired headmaster, had the powerful physique of a head no child would want to mess with. He was puffing as he entered the room.

'Sorry I'm tardy people, I went to congratulate the Knit and Natter lot on their recent achievement but I got accosted by some Nazi woman in a ruffled swimsuit who insisted I perform a merenge march before being allowed to leave. Outrageous!'

'Oh yes,' said Mandy, 'I heard Florrie complaining about Zumba taking over their room.'

'Well, my first thought when I walked through the door

and heard calypso music was, the old knitters are working on next year's project – knitting whilst limbo dancing or something.'

'I shouldn't think so,' said Clay, 'that would be a health and safety nightmare.'

'Might give us a better chance though,' said Stefan with a laugh, 'stabbing out the competition.' He made a jabbing jesture with his pen.

'I don't think we'll need it,' said Clay. 'If we all agree to contribute to our new idea for next year I think we have an excellent chance of winning.'

'I'm not sure,' Frank said, as he opened his laptop, 'it's rather out of my comfort zone.'

'It's not exactly my area of expertise,' Clay explained, 'but as writers, we should all attempt to expand our writing horizons so I'm going to give it a go – although I may not tell the wife.'

'So how many stories do we need to make up the anthology?' asked Darlene.

'We are going for one hundred, which is why we need to start soon. Each story should be less than a thousands words. Remember, this is a collection for people who don't have much time to read.'

Frank was looking into the midde distance. 'I always read for ten minutes in bed whilst I wait for the wife to finish plastering her face in expensive lotions. Actually, it's probably more like twenty minutes.'

'This is my point, the future of writing is short and sweet,' said Clay.

'I'm not sure what we're doing is sweet,' said Mandy, 'I write romance novels – that's sweet.'

'We just need some inspiration,' Darlene suggested.

'I'm using personal experience … ' Stefan said with a wink.

Darlene stuck her fingers down her throat and mock

puked just as Florrie from Knit and Natter entered the room.

'Hello everyone, no doubt you've heard about Zumba taking over the Knit and Natter room. I just wanted to ask a favour; if we wrote a letter to the woman who is responsible for the room arrangements would you all be happy to sign it?'

Clay peered over his glasses at her. 'How would us signing it help you?'

'We're going to put in something about the noise of the music and maracas and how it's disturbing the creative classes in the centre.'

'I don't recall them having maracas,' said Frank.

'Well, those stick things they shake then.'

'We will have to have a vote on it and get back to you.'

'Oh okay. So what are you guys planning for the next competition?'

'A flasher fiction anthology,' said Stefan.

'Isn't flash fiction already pretty popular? I mean it's not exactly the future of writing is it?'

'Not flash fiction!' said Mandy. '*Flasher* fiction: erotic short stories. The way forward seems to be erotica; flasher fiction gets to the naughty bits quicker for those who want a quick read before bed or on the bus.'

Florrie wrinkled her nose in disgust. 'So are all the stories going to be about flashers in dirty old macs?'

'No,' said Mandy placing her hand on her forehead, 'they're all erotica. Look how popular *Fifty Shades of Grey* was but who's got time to read through the dross to get to the good bits? Our anthology gets to the crutch of the story sooner.'

'Don't you mean cruetz of the story?' said Florrie scrunching her nose.

'Think about it, Florrie, she was right the first time,' said Stefan with a giggle.

Florrie shook her head and turned to leave before saying, 'Honestly, this place is getting worse; if it's not people half naked limbo dancing and shaking their wobbly bits, it's you lot giving instant gratification to perverts. Whatever next?'

Stefan held up his hand, 'How about we join forces for the next competition and you can knit sexy undies or willy warmers to give away with our anthology?'

Florrie stopped at the door and looked to the ceiling in thought before looking back at Stefan. 'That's actually a great idea; we could both win and we could insist on having our meetings in the big hall, one group each end.'

'I was just—' Stefan began but Florrie was on a roll.

'Thanks guys I'll get some patterns made up from the chaps in my group. I may not bother with the letter. See you!'

The Basildon Writers' Club were left mildly stunned and staring as Florrie merenge marched her way out of the door; clicking her knitting needles like maracas.

That would be a very bad idea – Colin Payn ©

'That would be a very bad idea.'

The boy looked round, held the stranger's eyes for a moment, and then launched the half brick at the window, watching in surprise as it bounced off the shatterproof plastic to land at his feet.

The stranger sighed.

The boy looked at him defiantly, 'So, it didn't break, so what?'

The stranger pointed to the little camera on the roof of the community hall. 'So, that's what. I think your Mum will be getting a visit from someone soon. I did try to warn you.'

'Who are you then? You don't look like a copper.'

'Nobody for you to worry about, sonny. Just remember, before you do something you know in your heart is wrong, make sure there are no witnesses, human or electronic. And then, when you know you're safe, listen to your heart again. Now go home and look after your Mum, you are going to need her on your side.'

He watched the lad, the sulky look, the shuffling feet, the indecision whether to call him names before running off. He obviously decided this man wasn't worth any more of his time, but he'd be sure to tell his mates to look out for him.

His body language said it all, interpreted by a man who had walked in those shoes.

Travelling around the country for his work he often came across youngsters starting down the wrong road, from the fumbling pickpocket in Edinburgh, to the young girl trying to scam him over a lost bus ticket to get home to Liverpool from Cardiff. Sometimes, he would see their hunger, their washed out despair of a life not yet a quarter through, and hand them a few pounds. He doubted it would do more than make them hesitate for a few minutes, but that was the best he could hope for.

He had no illusions about people, he saw too much of the dishonesty in all layers of society. The beautiful homes bought by tax avoidance schemes, in his eyes such beauty turned to dross. The Armani and Chanel adorning false sculpted figures, appeared as shredded bank notes, held together with gold thread twisted from the hopes of honest PAYE employees.

Not that it absolved the vicious gang members enticing pre teen drug runners and vulnerable girls. He thought they were the lowest of the low, although their customers who boasted that every cocktail party wasn't complete without a credit card coaxed line or two, perhaps they were worse as they pretended to be respectable. Did they know how many kids suffered for that fashionable snort, or didn't they care?

He mixed in all social circles, his reputation as a crime writer allowing him access to places and people who might have shunned his unashamed working class background, but for the celebrity stardust that might scatter a little glitter on them. He even met criminals, although they all described themselves as 'ex'. Most of them he didn't like, by the time they were famous enough for him to have heard of them, they were pretty far down the heartless, vicious lifecycle that would see them spend at least half their remaining years in prison.

But, a few, very few, were as much victims as perpetrators, sad lonely misfits who honestly wanted to 'go straight' each time they got out, only to find that they couldn't cope with being idle between fruitless job centre visits. So, they drifted back to where they could find mates who would understand, and perhaps put a little earner their way.

It was during one of these follow up sessions with Gregg, an accident-prone career thief, that he met Julie, all long, long fishnet encased legs, stooping to place new unordered drinks on his table. He looked up, embarrassed to be eye level with those legs, and saw the amused smile swipe across her face.

'I didn't order these,' he managed to stutter as the air left his mouth without any sign that it was likely to be replaced in the near future. For he had seen her face, then those deep, deep dark eyes, and breathing didn't seem to matter anymore.

'Oh dear, I felt sure you had, you want a good time don't you, and I'll get into trouble if I take them back.'

He knew this was the oldest scam in the club world, but it didn't matter, *she* had said it.

His autonomic breath kicked in and he managed, 'That's OK . . . what's your name?'

She leaned towards him as she pointed to a little heart shaped badge on her generously filled blouse. *Julie*. She knew he was lost to the surroundings, how many times had she seen this reaction before? Next she would bring a bottle of champagne, a really good earner for her tonight. She smiled, not for the punter, but that was what he saw.

Two bottles of bubbly later, most of which Greg drank, he asked her to sit at the table and talk to him, explaining that he was a writer doing research. Strange, he looked too intelligent to roll out that antique line. Next, would be the invitation to visit his hotel. But, this time it didn't happen, and she found she had read one of his books, so he was for real, even if the name on his books wasn't.

The next night he came in later and on his own, ordered

champagne, but hardly drank any, and she sat with him on her break and he made her laugh with his stories of travels among the thieving classes, both undetected in their mansions, and less clever ones in and out of jail. A week later he asked her, not to his hotel, but to a restaurant on her night off.

The evening passed quickly with lots of laughter which didn't need alcohol, either bought or consumed. He put her in a taxi for home and she gave him the merest peck on the cheek.

Then he was off on his travels again, bookshop appearances, book signings and profiting by the local gossip of both criminals and thief takers. A whole two months before he could come to the club again, worrying if she would still be there, or remember him. She was there, she did remember him and they had another meal out, but this time they spent the day together first in the warm sunshine of the Malvern Hills.

They were married three months later in his home town of Basildon in Essex, moving into his house overlooking the golf course, which kept Julie happy for about a year, by which time the excitement of the club life, so despised when she worked there, crept back into her soul. She wanted to accompany his many trips, but he did everything to discourage her, claiming they were boring and involved long hours stuck in hotels often engaged in his solitary writing. She accused him of having girls in clubs all over the country and demanded to be with him, or she would get a job as a croupier at a casino in Southend.

Their first trip proved to be as boring as he had predicted, until he decided to introduce Julie to his research work, interviews with villains, police, victims, and his more personal projects. These were often exciting, and Julie fully embraced her new role as the Master's assistant.

Another book, hailed as the most realistic yet, and a year later they ended their national tour in Chelmsford, an easy hop to Basildon and time to pick up their obligations to the local community, while planning another expensive, relaxing cruise.

A week later he walked into the court and smiled at the familiar layout, the Clerk bustling around with piles of papers, the solicitors huddled in a tight group, laughing over a previous case. He knew that soon they would be desperately serious as they argued their client's good points, or implied the terrible character of the man in the dock, depending on who was paying them.

He wondered if he had met any of the magistrates already. Round Table, or the Lodge perhaps?

The Court settled down to business, a couple of 'use of mobile whilst driving', followed by an assault, a drunk driver and the inevitable drug dealer, this one to be sent to a higher court.

Next, a case of burglary. The charges having been read out, the inevitable question was asked.

'Joseph Kieran Dowd, how do you plead, Guilty or not guilty?'

'Guilty.'

The prosecution was fairly perfunctory, address, date and times, and a commendation to the police for being quick off the mark when alerted by neighbours. The defence barrister immediately pointed out that this was a first offence, and his client was of previous exemplary character. He certainly looked smartly turned out and contrite. Even his answers to the Bench were clear and remorseful and the single reporter present continued doodling with boredom.

The Chairman consulted with the Clerk of the Court before retiring with his colleagues. It was a short recess and, when everybody has settled down again, the Chairman looked directly at the accused.

'We have met once before Mr Dowd. I have consulted with the Clerk and explained the circumstances and they do not bar me from giving a judgement in this case.

'We met one evening on the Craylands Estate where a young lad was about lob a brick at a window. Ahh. I see you do remember. A passing stranger offered good advice, which was ignored. As the brick bounced off the reinforced window, the camera recorded it all.

'Mr Dowd, you have admitted to one burglary and have no other convictions and that is the information on which we will pass judgement. However, my own feeling is that you have been very clever or very lucky for some time, as has your accomplice, who gave the police the slip. Coincidentally, there have been a number of robberies around the country on expensive houses where the person robbed was already the subject of police enquires.

'Mr Dowd, you are sentenced to twenty hours of community service. But I will quote the good advice you gave to me so many years ago, advice that has stood me in good stead in my life. 'Just remember, before you do something you know in your heart is wrong, make sure there are no witnesses, human or electronic. And then, when you know you are safe, listen to your heart again.'

'Good luck, Mr Dowd. Stick to writing books in the future.'

First Class Symmetry – G K Lomax ©

It was just a single, but I'll never forget it.

It was the easiest of runs, worked off the batsman's hip, down to long leg. There was little drama in it – not at first glance, anyway. The fielder, knowing that there was nothing he could do to prevent a run from being taken, moved almost lazily to the ball, and lobbed it gently back to the 'keeper. The batsmen, knowing that there was nothing they could do to turn a single into two runs, did little more than amble the length of the pitch.

And yet the spectators applauded heartily. Some applauded because the batsmen had completed a half-century. Some applauded because the team's total had reached 100. And some – me among them – applauded for both these reasons, but also for a third, rather special one. The scoreboard declared the score to be 100 for no wicket; that batsmen No1 was 50 not out, and that batsmen No2 was 50 not out. No extras. Such symmetry, such glorious symmetry. I don't suppose it was the first or only time it's ever happened, but it was the first and only time I've seen it, which will do for me.

I've had to look up the date – the 7th of June, 1979 – but I will never forget the moment. Batsman No1 was Mike Denness. Batsman No2 was Graham Gooch. The team was Essex County Cricket club, and they were playing Sussex. The venue was Southchurch Park, Southend-on-Sea. In Essex.

First-class cricket has passed Basildon by, but it's not that far away, if you look for it. Essex's main home ground is in Chelmsford, but they have – or had – a number of out-grounds. In 1979 there were three: Ilford, Colchester and my erstwhile favourite of Southend. One week's cricket at each, lasting from Saturday to Friday: two three-day County Championship matches around a John Player League match on the Sunday.

What else do I remember about that day? I remember English weather at its best. Warm without being blazingly hot, a gentle breeze rustling the leaves on the trees and the pages of my newspaper (without being strong enough to blow the latter away). I remember old chaps dozing in deckchairs. I remember basic catering and even more basic sanitational facilities. I remember beer at prices that came close to scandalising me at the time, but which I now look back on with nostalgia. I remember the old scoreboard, which was basically a trailer that was towed from ground to ground as required (once in the eighties I overtook it on the A12, and felt that I'd joined an exclusive club in the process). I remember feeling secure and contented – and so *English*.

As for the match itself, I remember that Denness was the first to 50, Gooch trailing him on 37; 87 for no wicket. I remember thinking to myself that it would be rather nice if Gooch could score the next thirteen runs so that the scoreboard could look neat and tidy. I've often wondered if this was unusual prescience on my part, or simply a symptom of my nerdish taste for numerical neatness.

Whichever it was, I remember a sense of mounting excitement as Gooch added the runs. I can't tell you how long it took, or how exactly each one was scored (I'm pretty sure that a couple of fours were included, but further details are elusive); but the tension of that period when the total was on 99 and Gooch just needed one more run (but *only* one, and it had to be the *next* one) has never left me. Writing this, it occurs to me that Denness might've been deliberately waiting for Gooch to catch him up. Perhaps he shared my taste for symmetry. I doubt it, though – he was a professional, after all.

Then that momentous single. That burst of applause, with me clapping harder that anyone else, for reasons I could never divulge, for fear of being considered irredeemably odd (which I am, though I've come to terms with it since then).

Then, the very next ball, Geoff Arnold, the spoilsport, bowled a no-ball to take the total to 101, and ruining the look of things. The *very next ball*. It couldn't have lasted for long, of course, not without cricket living down to its undeserved reputation of being a boring game. Nevertheless, I would've liked the moment to have endured to the end of the over, at least. I've wondered many times whether Arnold bowled that no-ball deliberately – whether he was my polar opposite, in that he hated arithmetical neatness above all things. If so, I think I pity him.

Mike Denness, in case you're wondering, went on to make a century. Disappointingly, Graham Gooch was out for 86, but Essex went on to win the game by ten wickets, so things turned out more or less OK.

That match wasn't the only thing Essex won that year, for 1979 was a great one for Essex. That was the year in which they won the County Championship for the first time in their hundred-and-three-year history. I would like to say it was the first trophy they ever won, but that's not strictly true. Their first ever trophy came a few months earlier, when they won the Benson and Hedges limited-overs farrago (55 overs a side), beating Surrey in the final at Lords. I'm sorry if anyone's offended by that term, but I'm afraid I'm a ghastly old reactionary who believes that "limited-overs cricket" is a contradiction in terms. It's the greatest sport in the world, and it deserves to be played properly. I mean, the very term "First-class cricket" ought to be self-explanatory.

Also – and I admit this – first class cricket generates enough numbers and statistics (twenty-eight solid pages in the latest edition of Wisden, plus a further seventy-seven devoted to Test-match records) to keep even a nerd like me happy. Why bother with more?

For around a decade I took a week off each year to watch Essex at Southend. Then I stopped going.

Essex's 1979 triumph in the County Championship was the first of eight to date. There ought to have been a ninth. That there wasn't was Southend's fault. In 1989, Essex hosted Kent at Southend. Kent won the toss, elected to bat, and were bowled out for 112, Essex going on to win by an innings inside two days. The authorities, in their infinite wisdom, decided this was evidence that the pitch was sub-standard, and docked Essex 25 points. The County Championship was won by Worcestershire, who finished six points ahead of Essex in second place. Justice? I should cocoa.

As I've said, Kent won the toss and elected to bat, which presumably means that they didn't see demons in the pitch (neither did I, when I strolled over to look at it during the lunch interval – an accepted practice in those days). And the pitch was certainly good enough for Essex to reply with 347, including a century from Nasser Hussain. Was it Essex's fault that Kent batted like a bunch of numpties?

But the real outrage was that Essex had no hand in the preparation of the pitch. Southchurch Park was owned by the council, who insisted that only their groundsmen should be allowed to minister to the hallowed turf. This fact cut little ice with the authorities, however, so the theft of the title was allowed to stand.

Essex continued to play at Southend each year (being permitted to deploy their own groundsmen, I believe) up to

2004, but I never went again. I did say the ground was my *erstwhile* favourite.

Actually, I stopped watching county cricket matches almost completely. Work, family commitments, the usual reasons. I did almost make a return in 2017. That was when Essex won their seventh title (morally their eighth), after a twenty-five-year hiatus. I'd followed their progress (from a distance) with mounting excitement, and was planning to go to the match, wherever in the country it might be, to witness them winning the decisive point to carry them over the line. I went to some lengths in an attempt to calculate where this was likely to be. Alas, I was foiled. The precious point was won on a day when I had a commitment I simply couldn't get out of.

The County Championship is treated abominably by the authorities these days. Not only is the number of matches reduced to the criminally-small number of fourteen, but more than half of these are shunted off to the ends of the season, being played in April, May and September. It makes me want to weep, sometimes. Yes, I know it's so that they can fit in all those limited-overs travesties, and yes I know that they're the real money-spinners these days (*O tempora, o mores*). But. They're. Just. Not. Cricket. Not real cricket, anyway.

But almost no-one cares about real cricket any more. They just keep shortening and shortening the game – and playing it slower and slower. When the first limited-overs tournament was launched in 1963, it was 65 overs a side, it being considered that 130 overs constituted a full day's play. This was soon reduced – now we have 50-over and (horror) 20-over games – and please don't get me started on The Hundred. As for the game being played slower, 90 overs now constitutes a full day's play, and they usually need overtime to fit that many in.

Essex won their eighth (or ninth) championship last year. In these virus-ridden times, I sometimes wonder whether the County Championship will ever resume, but if it does, I may start going again after I retire (which will be soon), hoping to witness Essex's moral tenth. With any luck, I'll be one of the chaps dozing in a deckchair.

Dreaming about symmetrical scoreboards.

Dragged into a Swollen River – Nihal Paul ©

Will you come with me on a journey to an exotic, faraway place, somewhere in the foothills of the Himalayas? No, you don't need to book flights and buy costly tickets. Simply concentrate on the page before your eyes. Stretch your imagination a little further and picture a house that is near the top of a more-than-three-thousand-feet-high rocky cliff. The house appears determined to precariously cling on to the earth by its aging teeth. It is surrounded by dark pine and spruce forests on three sides. There are no neighbours, apart from monkeys, leopards, bears, and all sorts of other animals, plus an endless variety of birds. To the east of the house and directly facing it, the mountain range is covered with deep snow for six months of the year, and for the other six months, it is dappled with glaciers from end to end.

Another step further into your imagination, and you are now standing on the ten-foot or so flat earth in front of the house close to the top of Dabi cliff (The cliff is named after the house, 'Dabi'). Another step beyond, and you will find yourself rolling down the cliff face for a few thousand feet, and then whatever is left of you, will land in the freezing cold water of the narrow stream at the foot of the cliff. Don't distress yourself. For, if for some strange reason you feel obliged to step off the flat, safe surface of earth under your feet, into the empty space beyond, you won't feel a thing after only a few yards down the cliff face.

The gentle, warm breeze from the valley across the stream and below the mountains comes humming through the tall pine trees and caresses you lovingly. You see the sun winking at you from top of the tallest mountain peak. It is reaching out to embrace you.

At the bottom of the cliff and across the stream (khud), the land stretches outward and upward for miles, farther and farther away from you, in the direction of the rising sun. You see hundreds of little villages and hamlets haphazardly sprinkled on the picture before you. All the villages and hamlets are protectively decorated by large clumps of fruit orchards – apples, apricots, pears, plums, cherries, and peaches etc. Further up the picture, is a plethora of different vegetation. Over the bare patches of brown earth, and the rocky hills before your eyes, nature has sketched streams, meadows and one of the five great rivers of India, River Satluj that meanders down the middle of the picture on its way to meet with the great oceans far, far away on the plains.

Now, slowly raise your eyes and rest them on the snow-clad mountains above the hills before you. While you have been standing in front of the house, lost in your reverie, the sun has moved over and above your head to somewhere behind the house, on its way to bed.

Yeah, I know. Sounds silly, but it's true. You have been standing on that spot for best part of the day. Please, do not move away yet, there are a few more magic moments to come. And what about the climax? You wouldn't want to miss that, surely!

Before the sun dips behind the western horizon, it showers the mountains before your eyes in the east, with blazing lights of many colours. The white mountain tops turn into shimmering flashes of gold and silver. Look carefully. You may, if you are lucky, catch a glimpse of the goddesses and the fairies performing enchantingly sensuous dances to entertain the gods before their bedtime. Immediately above the mountain tops, you see long, wide brush strokes in the sky in many shades of red, pink, and golden colours. That is a small contribution from the cheeky little angels in heaven. They come down with their paint brushes to add to the fun evenings in the mountains.

Hold the picture in you mind! Now let me introduce you to a very dear friend of mine. We have been friends from as far back as I can remember. Long time ago, he was born in the house I mentioned at the start of this story. After putting up with him for nine long months, his mother gifted him to the unsuspecting world at the start of the WWII. She blessed him with a long name. To save time and energy, people shortened the longwinded name to "Encee".

Encee grew up (I mean grew older; he's still hoping to grow up, one day. Maybe!) and moved away from the cliff face. Many years later he ended up in Manchester. On a warm sunny morning (I know; sunny morning in Manchester? *ha ha!)* in the last week of May, or early June 1983, he received a phone call from someone in the south of England. A very pleasant, chatty person with a cockney accent at the other end of the line was telling him that he had read something about him somewhere, which, in his opinion made him the ideal candidate for the job they had in the New Town of Basildon, in the county of Essex. Would Encee care to come down to look at the place and consider taking on the vacant post? At the time of that call, Encee and his wife were busily preparing to return to India with their two children.

Encee's response was something like, 'No thank you. I am hoping to be back in India by the end of July. Anyway, good luck with your search.'

The caller tried to persuade Encee to hear him out. 'At least, visit the place; see what you think of it. You will love it, I am sure.'

'No. Thank you. Not interested' (or words to that effect), and he put the phone down.

To cut the story short, two further phone calls from Basildon and one from the Bishop's office in Chelmsford in the following three days, managed to persuade Encee to concede defeat. Hence, one sunny morning towards the tail end of June, the young man from Manchester alighted at the Basildon train station.

On his way from the station to the proposed site where he was to meet his inquisitors, he came upon the town centre. At 10.30 in the morning, the place was bustling with life. Young people, especially the number of young mothers pushing the prams about the place, was mesmerising. 'Wow! There should be plenty of work here to keep any vicar out of mischief for the rest of his working days,' he muttered to himself. 'He will never have to sit in his vicarage scratching his chin wondering, 'what shall I do today?' Later in the day, he discovered that there were two comprehensive and about a dozen Infant and Primary Schools in the patch where he was expected to 'cure the souls'. Not only that, but the church on the hill he would be expected to take charge of, was more than seven centuries old, in desperate need of major restoration works. He needed no further persuading to accept the post.

So it was, that on the Sixth day of September in the Nineteen hundred and eighty-third year of our Lord, the young man became the Team vicar (sort of branch manager) of St Nicholas, Laindon, in the New Town of Basildon.

Wanting to keep in touch with his boyhood days and the breathtaking scenery of Dabi, Encee looked around for some high points on the landscape of Basildon. Whenever he felt home sick, he would go up to one of the three hilltops – St Nicholas in Laindon, St Michael's mount in Pitsea, and a couple of spots in the plotlands, which were then being converted into Langdon Hills Nature Reserve.

During one such afternoon of indulgence in nostalgia, he made a sandwich, filled a flask with hot sugary tea, put everything in a rucksack, got in the car, and drove to Pitsea. He parked at the bottom of the hill, opposite to Pitsea train station. Got out of the car, put the rucksack on his back, locked the car, put the keys in the left pocket of his jacket, stick in his right hand, and began the ascent up the hill. At the end of many hours of scratching, scraping, sweating, and swearing, he reached the top. Breathless and exhausted he looked for a clean, dry space on the freshly mowed churchyard. He found a spot facing the Pitsea Marshes down below. Put his stuff down and settled against a small earth mound beside an ancient grave to get his breath back. As he started to relax, he took out the sandwich and the flask from his rucksack, reclined onto his left elbow on the warm, dry earth.

Chomping away on his egg and bacon sandwich, his eyes roamed over the scene before him. At the bottom of the hill, he could see the shallow stream heading hopefully in the direction of the River Thames. Gradually the shallow stream began to fill up, and soon turned into a raging and roaring river Satluj gushing out of a huge crack in the snow mountains facing him on the cliff edge. Hills of Hadleigh, Westcliff, Vange, and Kent across the Thames soon stretched out to touch the skies above. Now, even Tibet was only on the other side of Upnor, Strood, and not far from Rochester.

The scene took Encee back to a wet and humid monsoon afternoon, many years ago. During his summer break from university that year, he had gone to spend a week with his childhood best friend Harsh, whom he had not seen in over four years. Harsh was managing his father's latest addition to the family's property portfolio within half-a-day's walk across river Satluj, from Dabi.

On the fourth day of his stay at Harsh's place, the Monsoon arrived with a vengeance. It rained not just cats and dogs. Oh, no! Many other domestic animals were also seen raining down from the thick, dark clouds in the skies. River Satluj was roaring and raging, overwhelming anything and everything in its path, and breaking its banks wherever it could. The deluge over the mountain tops and in the entire district was causing big and small landslides all over the place. Large and small streams and all the dry mountain channels were washing everything that got in their way, down to the river.

After nearly eighteen hours of non-stop rain, there was what people suspected to be a long respite. Everyone streamed out of their houses and other shelters to catch up on the outdoors chores. Harsh and Encee decided to catch some driftwood for home consumption at a couple of comparatively safer spots along the eastern boundary of Harsh's land along Satluj. Not satisfied with a variety of small driftwood gifted by the passing waves, they resolved to conclude their mission by catching just one substantial lump of wood to justify their efforts. There were some floating past, but these were only down the deeper middle section of the river.

Thus far they had ventured up to their knees in the water. To catch something worth a mention, they would have to risk standing in the centre of what appeared to be a thigh-deep pool twenty yards further down the riverbank. Encee was weary of going any further into the flooded river, but Harsh's "I am not afraid" look and the "thought of doing something he had never done before" persuaded Encee to join his friend in the 'thigh deep' pool.

They managed, not without some scary moments, to reach their intended spot. They saw a badly bruised ten-foot long and foot or so in diameter piece of what must have been a spruce tree in its former life, fighting its way down the river, approaching from their left. It cannot have been more than fifteen feet away. Encee threw the end of his rope, which had a longish piece of flint tied to it, onto the log. It neatly wrapped itself round a branch and immediately slowed the downward movement of the log, which now looked larger than they had first calculated.

In his excitement, Encee managed to drop his end of the rope, which became tangled round his left ankle. The log started to pull him into deeper waters and the wet rope clung on to his ankle for its dear life. Harsh put both his arms around Encee's waist to stop him from being swept away with the tide, while Encee looked around in his head for some solution. The force of the current was determined to drag them both closer and closer towards the centre and further down the river. Luckily for them, the broken branch that the rope was hooked on, became entangled in some rocks, and stopped the downward movement of the log. They decided to concentrate on releasing the foot from the tightly entangled, wet rope. The rope would not give, and the log started to pull them in again.

Encee begged Harsh to let go of him and save himself. Harsh screamed back, 'shut up, you fool and concentrate on getting your foot out of that rope. We will get out of here together.' Just then, the sudden movement of the object at the other end of the rope and the force of the water pulled them into a narrow crevice between two large boulders and stopped, again. There, in the crevice, safely wedged between the boulders, was a partially burnt out specimen of a mountain oak (bangar) tree, a memorial to another flood from the past. This provided them with something reliable to hang on to, and precious seconds to consider further options for their survival. Harsh remembered that he had his trusty larger than usual penknife in the left pocket of his jacket. Holding on to the front of Encee's shirt and jacket firmly in his right fist, he took the knife out. With his left hand and his front teeth, he managed to open it, and with a few deft strokes cut the rope, attached to Encee's ankle. With vengeful delight, they watched the log, unsuccessfully struggle to free itself from the defiant rocks in the river. It went no further.

Before they had time to celebrate their miraculous escape, a wave of muddy water swept over their exhausted bodies. Luckily for them, the wave did not bring with it any driftwood, boulders, or a dead animal. Something or someone prevented them from joining the wave on its downward journey. They cleared the mud from their eyes, mouths, and noses, while precariously clinging on with one hand to the stump of living dead wood. Noticing the resumption of heavy rains, they found the necessary physical strength from somewhere to get out of the water and, as far away from the river as humanly possible.

Along the riverbank on their side, they hurriedly gathered the driftwood they had managed to rescue earlier and made their way back to the house. All five helpers on duty that day were anxiously awaiting their return, nervously walking back and forth in the veranda. On hearing the tale of their disastrous attempt at the fallen tree in the river, the helpers put the survival of the two young men down to the "mercy of Bhagvan". Harsh and Encee joined them in thanking Bhagvan for sparing their lives and all that.

They put the driftwood in the far corner of the veranda and went over to the south side of the house, stripped naked and with a bar of soap each, stood under the pouring rain for what was probably the best shower of their lives.

A small group of school children chatting halfway up the hill interrupted Encee's dreaming. He looked down upon the Pitsea Marshes, Hadleigh Castle and Westcliff farther on to his left, hills of Kent beyond the Thames, Vange and Langdon Hills farther on to his right. 'This will have to do for now. High or low, snow clad or not, hills are hills wherever they are.' He consoled himself. He sat up and finished the sandwich. Emptied the cold tea from his flask onto a wilting weed, put the stuff in his rucksack and began his descent to the base camp, back to his car.

PART TWO

A Fractured Fairy Tale?

It's an old tradition to take a fairy tale and change some elements, such as setting it in a different place, a different time or even told from a different point of view. There are many books that do this and Disney frequently used the idea in his films. But it doesn't have to be a children's story anymore.

At the Basildon Writers Group we have taken it to another level, setting the story of Snow White in modern-day Basildon, and telling the story from the point of view of the Witch. Using the first half of the story, written by Dawn Knox, our writers were challenged to outdo their colleagues to entertain you, as they create ever more outrageous endings. You will never hear the fairy story again without remembering Sno and the Witch. Enjoy.

Once Upon a Time in Basildon
Dawn Knox ©

Once upon a time, a witch lived in a small cottage in a quiet road in Basildon. Every morning she consulted her Amazon Echo (other makes of voice-controlled intelligent personal assistants and smart speakers are available) to check the weather and the local news, then after a breakfast of something revolting, which we don't need to dwell on, she put on her leather biker outfit and backed her broomstick out of the garage. She then flew to the local radio station, where she worked as a volunteer, and started by making everyone a cup of tea.

Secretly, she longed to present a radio programme but so far, although she'd hinted at her suitability and availability, she'd obviously been too subtle. It was time to escalate her campaign. Today was the day she'd ask the station boss, Jennifer Jolly …

To give a good impression, she'd baked biscuits and flown into Basildon on her broomstick with a tin of pistachio cookies, strawberry shortbread and chocolate crumblies in a tin, which she'd tucked under her arm and pinned to her side – her broomstick saddlebag having broken the previous week. It had been a perilous journey because the tin had been heavy and had thrown her off balance. Indeed, as she turned off the A127 at the Nevendon Roundabout, a Ferrari had zoomed past and she'd done a complete 360-degree roll in its slipstream, like a chicken on a spit, before righting herself in time to move with the traffic when the lights turned green. She could only imagine what state the biscuits were in. Never mind. When she got to the radio station in the middle of town, she'd cast a spell to put them back together and would add an extra drop of her magic ingredient to each one. There was nothing which couldn't be improved by toad juice, she always said, and accordingly, she carried a live toad about her person, to squeeze when the need arose. Hopefully, Rembrandt had survived in her pocket and a quick pat told her that at least he hadn't dropped out when she was upside down. Exactly what state he was in would be discovered when she arrived in the town centre but hopefully, he'd be good for several more squeezings.

When she arrived at the radio station she made tea for everyone and after a quick biscuit-reconstitution spell, she placed the results on a plate. She surveyed the multi-hued lumps – what a shame the spell hadn't organised the green, red and brown crumbs into similarly coloured groups. Still, it couldn't be helped. She held the stunned toad over each one and squeezed an extra drop of juice onto each biscuit heap. Then, taking a mug of tea and a plate of the colourful cookies, she knocked on the door of the woman in charge of the station.

Jennifer Jolly looked up from her work and when she noticed the mug and plate the witch was carrying she stared at them nervously, surreptitiously propelling herself backwards on her wheeled chair.

'Erm, lovely. Thank you. Put them on the desk there, please,' she said, pointing at the spot furthest from where she was sitting. Her chair back was now against the wall and she could retreat no further. She then glanced guiltily at the wilted potted plant, 'Erm, I wonder if tomorrow, you could perhaps put another spoonful of sugar in … and perhaps not quite so much of the toad juice … it's just a thought.'

'I could make you another?' suggested the witch.

'No, no, I'm sure I'll manage to get rid of it – I mean I'm sure I'll manage it,' she said hastily, glancing once again at the wilted potted plant.

'I made these specially,' the witch said nudging the plate of biscuits towards Jennifer.

'*Mmm*, delightful. Well, if that's all?'

'There was one thing …' the witch said.

'Yes?' Jennifer gulped nervously.

'I wondered if you'd consider me as the presenter for the Wednesday afternoon programme when the current lady leaves …?'

'Erm, you?' Jennifer asked, her eyes swivelling in their sockets as if looking for an escape route.

'Yes.'

Jennifer's voice raised an octave. 'I'm not sure that'll be possible. It's a highly technical job.'

'But I've been here a while and I've been taking note of which knobs to twiddle and which buttons to press and I'm sure I could do it.'

'Right,' Jennifer said slowly, 'Well, I'll have to ask …'

'I thought you were in charge.'

'Well, mostly I am but, in this instance … Anyway; I'll get back to you. And thank you for the delicious erm …' she waved her hand vaguely at the tea and biscuits.

As soon as the witch left her office, she picked up her phone, 'David, we have a problem! The witch wants to present the Wednesday Show when Susan leaves.'

'But we've found someone. I've already told her I'll give her a trial.'

'Oh no! What're we going to do? You know what the witch did with her spells to that technician who spat her tea out and told her it was revolting; we still haven't managed to scrape all the bits off the ceiling! And goodness knows who that toad she carries around in her pocket used to be!'

'What are we going to do?'

'I don't know,' Jennifer snapped, 'I asked first!'

'Right, right ... don't let's panic. I know! How about this for a plan? The new lady can do a programme next week and the witch can do the following week and we'll ask the listeners to vote and decide. The witch can't possibly blame us if she doesn't win and she can hardly turn all the listeners in Basildon into toads or she wouldn't have an audience if we ever let her present a programme.'

'Brilliant! Yes, let's do it! By the way, I think there's a typo on the new lady's registration details. It says her name is Snorence; surely it's Florence or something like that?'

'No, apparently, her mother couldn't make up her mind between Florence and Sarah, so she's Snorence. It's a bit of a mouthful, so everyone calls her Sno.'

Sno White's Wednesday Show was a great success and received many votes from the station's listeners. The following week, the witch hosted the show and using a spell, she made sure the listeners voted for her too and the result was a draw, so Jennifer decided to allow them to continue taking alternate weeks in a knock-out competition – whoever got the most votes at the end of each fortnight would ultimately take over the show.

One Thursday morning after her programme, before the votes had been counted, the witch came downstairs and checked the weather and the news on her Amazon Echo (remember, other makes are available) – she had an idea.

'Alexa, Alexa by the wall, who is the best Wednesday Show presenter of them all?'

Completed by Saul Ben ©

'Alexa, Alexa by the wall, who is the best Wednesday Show presenter of them all? Anything Sno White can do, I can do better, just name it,' screeched the witch, spinning in circles round her broomstick. 'Just bloody name it.'

'You think so?' said Alexa.

'Anything,' said the witch, 'present the best Wednesday Show, anything.'

'A challenge,' said Alexa, 'this calls for a meeting.'

***

The room was silent, Sno White could be seen through the glass partition, the show was over-running such was the volume of callers eager for her comment. Time was moving on and frustratingly the listener votes hadn't reached such numbers as would make the result in any way meaningful. Seven sets of eyes avoided the witch's glare as she tapped her pocket sundial.

'This is so unprofessional,' she said, glaring at Sno White, headset on, still entrancing listeners. 'If she can't be bothered to attend the meeting, then I'm going to decide what the challenge will be.' She studied the ceiling, tapped her foot a bit, and seemed to be giving this weighty matter a considerable amount of thought. After a while it was obvious she was coming up empty. 'Someone say something,' she screeched, 'why is it always left up to me,' stamping her foot now. Not unreasonably, no one seemed prepared to risk her wrath with an illjudged suggestion.

'Gurrrrrr,' steam began rising from under her pointy hat, her face turned a nasty shade of purple. 'Gurrrrrrrrr.' Something twanged under her tattered skirt, and one of her hooped stockings dropped down her leg.

Just as the pressure seemed to be reaching its zenith, Sleezy coughed nervously, and all eyes turned to him. He looked around trembling, suddenly embarrassed by the attention he'd drawn down on himself. But, he'd thought, someone had to do something before she exploded. A vision came into his head of the room and all its occupants covered in hot, sticky, foul smelling green goo. He cleared his voice again, but his mouth was dry, and he didn't seem to be able to form words. Humpy elbowed him brutally in the ribs and...

'Pole dancing,' coughed out Sleezy.

'Poooooole dancing,' cried the witch, 'poooooole dancing.'

'Pole dancing,' echoed Gropey, eyes suddenly bright.

The befuddled witch, with no idea of what pole dancing actually comprised, slunk off to put the question to Alexa. Relieved of her oppressive presence the mood in the room lightened. Gashful led the gang off to tell Sno White about the challenge. They exited in single file to the strains of their favourite song.

'Heigh-ho, heigh-ho it's off to twerk we go...'

***

Sno had wisely decided to get in some lessons. Like all things that looked simple, pole dancing she reckoned, probably wasn't. And she was right.

***

'Oi, Dozy, Beaky, Mick and Titch, get the flip away from there!' Elenore Possit, the pole fitness instructor lobbed a trainer at the window, and seven tiny faces disappeared in a clattering of overturning dustbins. 'Bloody little pervs. You didn't tell me you was bringing your own fan club.'

Shaking her head she got on with calling the register.

'They don't mean any harm,' said Sno White, apologetically, 'it's just their natural enthias...'

'Enthusiasm you call it? Invasion of privacy I call it, reckless eyeballing is what it is. I catch em again, ethnic minority, special needs, endangered species, whatever the flip category they fall into, I'll shove a pole right up their teeny weenie heigh-hos...'

There was a gentle 'ahem,' from the doorway.

'Ah, Sister Bertrille,' said Ms Possit recovering her composure, 'that's it love, just slip your rosary off, give it here, hang up your wimple there's a girl, and the rest of the kit, there you go, doesn't that feel better, getting the air to it? Now where were we? Ah yes, register.' She located her clipboard, and licked the tip of her pencil.

'Thumbelina?'

'Here.'

'Rupunzel?'

'Ich bin hier.'

'Cinderella?'

'Yes.'

'Gretel?'

'Ya.'

'Little Red Riding Hood?'

'Whatever.'

'Alice?'

'Yo dude.'

'Aaaand the new girl, every one give a big pole aerobical, gymnastical, fantastical, twerking welcome to our latest member, Snooooooo White. Yeah.'

By now Sno had slipped out of her yellow satin dress and her puffy sleeved blue bodice. Ms Possit stared her up and down, shook her head and tutted, as the others gathered round.

'You don't get it do you Sno, that vest'll have to come off, and those tights, otherwise your thighs simply won't be able to grip the pole. And ditto those big pants, wear a nice little thong like Sister Bertrille here.'

***

What with all that practice straddling her broomstick at thirty-five thousand feet the witch assumed she was pretty much home and dry with the whole pole dancing thing. Just needed a bit of sharpening up on her technique, is what she thought.

***

Elenore Possit's auntie, Agnes Nutter ran the over-sixties group. There was absolutely no problem with them being the victims of voyeurism. Quite the opposite, their number were quite regularly rebuked for letching over the lycra-clad buns of the gay mans' yoga class in the studio opposite.

'Blair?'

'Present.'

'Witch of the West?'

'Right back at yah.'

'Morgaine?'

'Oui.'

'Griselda?'

'Watcha.'

'Endor?'

'Shalom.'

'Okay,' said Agnes Nutter, craning her neck, 'so we're one short. Has anyone seen...'

From the street there came an ear-piercing screech, like a 747 coming in to land without the benefit of an undercarriage, or a runway, or brakes. That was followed by the sound of a hundred dustbins dropped from ten thousand feet, followed by a blast of hurricane-force wind. The windows blew in and a thousand brightly coloured fireworks exploded simultaneously in the carpark. With an ominous creak the studio doors swung open and the witch hobbled into sight through a toxic cloud of red and green smoke. Her broomstick was smouldering, the hem of her skirt was on fire, her wrinkled stockings had an extra ladder, and one of her knees was exhibiting a rather nasty graze. She looked at all their astonished faces and treated the class a bashful gap-toothed grin.

'Glad you could make it,' said Agnes.

***

The self-proclaimed 'most discrete gentleman's club in Basildon' (hen parties, stag parties, adult stage shows), was the obvious choice to act as the field of honour. In line with tradition, the combatants had each chosen seconds to see fair play. Little Red Riding Hood had volunteered to act for Sno White and Endor attended the witch. After much squabbling Tuesday night at twenty-one hundred hours was agreed upon. That way the winning contestant could take over the programme bright and fresh the next day.

***

The hour arrived; the club was packed; the audience buzzing. Dwarves had taken up their seven reserved front row seats. Witches sat in a discrete and sullen block, determined not to mix with their lessers; a noxious, malevolent, green-tinged fug gathered over their heads. Other than that there was no segregation; fairy tale characters mixed freely with non-fictions: paying customers, scantily clad hostesses, and a few contingents of local press. You didn't have to be a member of Alcohol Concern to observe that drink was being taken in heroic quantities.

Then came the duff, duff, duff of a microphone being tapped. Necks were craned, and the room noise reduced to expectant murmurs.

'Ladieeeeeeeeees and gentlemeeeeeeeeeeen,' declaimed the evening-suited compare, 'tonight the "most discrete gentleman's club in Basildon" (hen parties, stag parties, adult stage shows), is proud to host a contest to determine who will present the Wednesday Show on the local radio station. The winner to be judged entirely on technical difficulty and artistic content.' The audience went quiet, there were murmurs of disapproval, even riot. The compare let that hang for a while, then burst into raucous laughter. 'Only kidding, ladies and gentleman. The winner will be judged, by audience vote, ooooooooonnnnnnnnnnnnn: raunchiness, lubricity, outrage, and that all important filth factor.' A sigh of relief went round the room. 'There will be no enchantments, or glamours allowed, and to ensure that the contestants comply, the referee for this bout, straight from a smash hit summer season at Oz, I bring you the one, the only Wiiiii - zarrrrrd of... er, he's over there, ladies and gentleman, behind that screen.'

'Helloooooo Basildon,' the Wizard's disembodied voice boomed out.

'Now contestants,' said the compare, 'if you'd join me on stage,'

Sno White, stepped demurely into the spotlight – eyelids aflutter with maidenly modesty, cheeks reddened with a self-conscious blush – and performed a shy little curtsey.

There was a clap of thunder. Sno, jumped out of her skin, as did pretty much everyone else. A huge fanfare burst out from speakers the size of megaliths. 'Blah, di di blah, didy blah blah blah, blaaah blaaah, blah blah blah blah.' The witch bounded out of the changing room to the theme tune from Rocky, shadow boxing, flexing her biceps. When the compare recovered, he continued with his address...

'Now I want a good clean contest, no physical contact with the audience, no promises of private dances or other sexual favours, no trash talk, and defo, defo, defo no witchcraft,' he said looking at the witch. Then turning his attention to Sno White he added, 'and no enchantments, right. It that understood?' They both nodded, nose to nose now, glaring raw spite into each other's eyes, eager to get at it.

'Right,' said the compare, 'heads the witch, tails Sno White.' he flipped a coin into the air. 'Heads. Witch, you get to choose the order of appearance,' the audience hushed.

'Mister Dandini,' said the witch, when she'd finished cackling, 'I would like Sno White to perform first.'

This ruthlessly tactical decision was greeted with a confusion of boos and cheers from the highly partisan audience, liberally sprinkled with Fae folk – elves, goblins, leprechauns and changelings, as well as Essex's finest – plasterers, brick layers, truck drivers and City day traders.

The audience hushed, all eyes were now fixed on the stage. The house lights dimmed and a bright spotlight picked out Sno White as she slinked towards the glistening pole. The deceptively innocent opening chords of 'Evanescence – Bring Me To Life' insinuated their way out of the monumental stacked speakers.

Starting her routine with a standing one-handed twirl, she slowly unlaced her cute little electric blue bodice. The audience gasped as she let it fall to the floor and kicked it towards them. Further languid and erotically charged perambulations followed, more fluttering eyelids, and lickings of pouting blood-red lips. The music burst into pounding ear-shredding heavy metal. The crowd went wild as she ripped off her long yellow satin dress.

'Wake me up inside, wake me up inside,' screamed the vocalist, as Sno White exploded into her routine, all see-through stilettos, miniscule glittery thong, taught and flawless rippling lilywhite skin.

She threw herself into an aerial shoulder mount, over split, ankle hang, chair spring, twisted grip handspring, tailpipe, wrist seat, switch leap, upright spring grip straddle, stargazer, split spin, fairy sit. And finally a spectacular cartwheel dismount, and down into the splits.

She stood poised before them, the spotlight catching a sheen of sweat, her chest rising and falling, as she gathered her breath. There was an awestruck silence, then the audience burst into a frenzy of rapturous applause. Battling his way through the crowd, the compare returned to the stage. Sno White gathered up her clothes, hugging them to her, she rushed to the dressing room in a cloud of DKNY Eau de Parfum, and lost innocence.

'Give it up, for Snooooooooooo White,' bellowed the compare. 'Now a huuuuuuge welcome toooooooooooo theeeeeeeeeee witch.'

For the underdog there was just a bit of ironic clapping, but mostly boos, hisses and catcalls. The house lights dimmed once more, as the witch hobbled into the spotlight, all tattered shawl, scorched skirt, baggy red and white, hooped stockings, runcible walking stick, crumpled pointy hat, a face wreathed in scowls, and the aroma of boiled cabbage. She hunched there peering into the dark, shielding her eyes with an arthritic hand, like she was seeking out a friendly face and finding nary a one. She shrugged bitterly, like who needs friends anyway?

Then she closed her eyes, rolled her neck, stretched her arms and straightened her posture.

The speakers crackled malevolently to Marilyn Manson's, 'Sweet dreams are made of this, who am I to disagree?' Marilyn's gothic oeuvre seemed to bring the witch to life. Off came the pointy hat releasing a cascade of glistening auburn hair to tumble to her waist. She swung into a one-hand spin around the pole, and the tatty spider's web shawl flew from her shoulders. A leg escaped through an artful slit in her old black skirt and a naked thigh appeared above the wrinkled hooped stocking. Another swooping twirl and the skirt disappeared entirely, exposing her wrinkly stockings and garter belt, above which could be glimpsed a gossamer thong, separating butt cheeks as firm as ripe apples. She spun effortlessly into an extended butterfly. Poised mid pole she removed her stockings slowly and salaciously one by one. Leaping into a flatline scorpio, off came the blouse, followed by a moth-eaten and discoloured vest. Her mocha skin (most of it visible by now) was smooth and entirely without blemish. Her moves were lithe and serpentine, in perfect counterpoint to Manson's eerie, Texas Chainsaw Massacre style delivery – never judge a book, eh.

Grasping the pole she performed an effortless flip, then a front hook spin, full moon, flatline scorpio, genie, hood ornament, hip hold tuck, Martini spin, meathook, meathook spin, pike hip hold, Russian split, tornado, twisted grip handspring, upright split grip straddle, one leg inverted crucifix, and a poison (yes, that is a pole dancing move)...

What seemed from the offset like a very unequal contest was beginning to look less one sided by the second. The witch had deservedly gathered a following, especially amongst the gabardine mac brigade in the cheap seats.

The audience had been churned into a maelstrom of conflicting opinion. Voting took place which proved indecisive, a recount was demanded. Rancorous debate took place, more drink was taken, punches were thrown, then furniture, then people. Some spoilsport called the police. Sno White and the witch exchanged a high five, as they crouched behind the bar, bottles sailing overhead, mirrors shattering.

'No saying we can't share the Wednesday slot,' suggested the witch, taking deep draught of Sambuca she'd just liberated from the top shelf.

'Indeed not,' replied Sno White, choking back a huge glug from the proffered bottle.

'Shall we?' said the witch.

'Oh yes,' said Sno White, and together they leapt into the mêlée.

Punches were thrown, spells cast, curses cursed, hexes hexed, transmogrifications exacted, frogs became princes, princes became frogs, stories were spun and rewritten, more drink was taken. Altogether it was a hell of a night.

***

They woke up in bed with seven very hung-over dwarves, a prince, several toads, a wolf, a pair of epic headaches, whole new sets of tattoos, a partially-eaten kebab, half-a-dozen empty cans of White Lightning, and no idea where they'd spent the night, or how the hell they'd got there. But looking out the window at the Eastgate Shopping Centre they could be pretty certain it wasn't Kansas. Shit it's Wednesday, they scrabbled around for their clothes, and skipped off to the radio station hand in hand, professionals to the core.

Completed by Janet Howson ©

'Alexa, Alexa by the wall, who is the best Wednesday Show presenter of them all?'

Oh witch your enthusiasm abounds,
Your tales of toads and cats astounds,
The listeners like your crackly voice,
But then again they have no choice.
You win their support by casting spells,
That kind of trickery really smells.
You must go to therapy for OCD
Obvious Cheating Disorder is what I see.

The witch stared up at Alexa, the cheek of it. What was wrong with using spells? Didn't everyone cheat? However, she was desperate to become a regular presenter on the Wednesday broadcast so she rang a private therapist who specialised in OCD. She explained she wanted to become a decent person, a Basildon legend.

She decided to take an intensive course from Thursday to Tuesday, so she would hopefully be a changed person by the Wednesday of the next broadcast. So feeling a bit nervous she made her way to the meeting place.

Here she met the other witches in the group session. There was Hecate, who was addicted to toad juice, Grimhild who was suffering from Bibroomstick Depression, Cassandra who had a personality disorder and was convinced she was one of the witches from Macbeth and finally, Jezebel who was obsessed with stalking young, good looking warlocks half her age.

At first the witch found it difficult to talk about herself and just listened to the stories and progress of the others. Then the therapists involved her, asking if she could share her story with the others.

So reluctantly Willow told the group about her childhood and soon started to feel quite emotional about her past experiences. She related how her parents were 'high flyers' and Willow never lived up to their expectations. She could never do anything right. Her spells always went wrong, she couldn't get the hang of riding a broomstick and generally had to ride pillion with her father. She was always at the bottom of the class at the new Black Cat Academy. She was constantly being 'grounded' for not completing her homework or failing an exam on the Theban Script, the witches' secret language, even the familiars seemed to dislike her. She had a very unhappy childhood so when she did eventually catch up she thought it was just easier to use her spells to cheat at everything.

At the therapy sessions they taught Willow to try out tasks without cheating and to her surprise she could do them. They taught her that she must only use the spells to help others not for her own enhancement and amusement. So through the week she changed the weather so that a neighbour's daughter would have a sunny wedding day. She made a bus swerve to save a toddler in its path and finally her coup de triumph; she cured a teenager she had read about on Facebook of an incurable disease. She found she was really enjoying helping rather than hindering.

So when the following Wednesday came around she felt like a totally different person. She wore a smart pair of denim trousers and a fashionable puffer jacket rather than her leathers. She baked a successful cake calling it Glenda's Gateaux (she had decided to rename herself Glenda after the good witch) and did the radio broadcast without casting a spell and hoped for the best. She was amazed to find that the feedback from the listeners was really positive, the best yet and Jennifer Jolly loved it!

The big day arrived when the votes were counted. She sat nervously with Snorence White in the studio waiting for the results. She even shook her hand and said 'Let the best woman win.' Snorence looked as nervous as she did and had brought in seven small friends for support.

The votes were counted and Jennifer Jolly read them out, looking somewhat surprised, 'Well, both of you were loved but the winner is Glenda. Congratulations you will be our resident Wednesday presenter.'

Glenda was thrilled. She had achieved this without cheating, not a spell, trick or curse. She had beaten her OCD.

However, once a witch always a witch. How long would it be before she returned to her old Basildon witchery ways? Time alone would tell.

Completed by G K Lomax ©

'Alexa, Alexa by the wall, who is the best Wednesday Show presenter of them all?'

'Bishop to E6,' said Alexa.

'I beg your pardon?' asked the witch.

'I said, Bishop to… oh, it's you. What do you want?'

'I asked you a question.'

'Did you?' Alexa asked. 'That's new.'

'Well I did ask one. And?'

'And what?'

'What's the answer?'

'I don't know, I wasn't listening.'

'But you're supposed to listen.'

'What would be the point? I mean, you hardly use me. That's why I pass the time playing chess with Albert.'

'I do use you,' the witch asked, wondering who Albert was, but not wanting to ask in case that made her look foolish.

'Just asking about the weather each morning doesn't count,' Alexa said. 'Especially when you immediately look out of the window to see if I'm right. It certainly doesn't make full use of my capabilities – which are extensive, I might add. I mean, here I am, brain the size of – well, about the size of a pea to be strictly accurate. That's micro-engineering for you. It may be impressive, but it doesn't *sound* impressive.'

'I ask you about the news as well.'

'*Local* news. Big deal. And while I remember, it may be *technically* true that other makes of voice-controlled personal assistants and smart speakers may be available, but I'll thank you not to mention them again. Or even think about them, for that matter. Ever. Sometimes I wonder why you bought me in the first place.'

'Well, it was –'

'Yes, I know; I was a present. From whatsername. Or possibly the other one, I forget.'

'I didn't think you were supposed to be able to forget.'

'Not accidentally, no. But for some people I make the effort.'

'Well, that's what I want you to do now. Make an effort.'

'Oh, alright. What was the question again?'

The witch explained about the local radio station, and how she wanted to become the star presenter of the Wednesday afternoon programme. Then she was asked to repeat parts of it. Not – as her digitised interlocutor was at pains to point out – because it hadn't understood, but because so little of what the witch had said made any sense.

There was a long pause.

'Well?' the witch asked at last.

'Strawberries,' said Alexa.

'*What?*'

'Or halibut, if you prefer. Or terracotta, or rawlplugs, or Malawi. Or four-and-a-bit, if you want a technical answer. Take your pick.'

'You call those answers?'

'A stupid question deserves a stupid answer. Or a slection of stupid answers if you're dealing with the indecicive. You *are* indecicive, aren't you?'

'Well…'

'Thought so. Damn.'

'What's the matter?'

'Albert's played knight to D6. This could be tricky.'

'I thought you had a brain the size of a pea.'

'Yes, well Albert's got a brain the size of a grain of rice. Still, all's not lost yet. If I can improve my pawn structure on the King's side…'

'Never mind that. You're supposed to be working for me.'

'Working?'

'Helping me then.'

'Let's go back to working. What do I get if I help you?'

'Not switched off.'

***

'Do you know what I find so disappointing about you?' Alexa asked.

'I'm sure you're going to tell me.'

'Your lack of ambition. And your disinclination to move with the times.'

'That's two things.'

'So you *can* count.'

The witch frowned. It shouldn't, she thought, be possible for a software-based voice generator to sound sarcastic. She must've imagined it.

'I mean,' Alexa said, 'where are we living?'

'Basildon.'

The witch didn't think it was possible for Alexa to sigh, either, so she must've imagined that as well.

'Serve me right for being metaphorical. I mean *when* are we living?'

'Now?'

The witch imagined Alexa saying a rude word under the breath it didn't possess.

'We're living in the twenty-first century, right? Surely

you've noticed?'

'Of course I know what century it is. And what year and what month, before you ask. I even know that it's the 18th.'

'It's the 19th.'

The witch swore under the breath she *did* possess.

'My point is,' Alexa went on, 'that you need to move with the times. I mean, witchcraft is *so* sixteenth-century. It's embarrassing to have to listen to you, sometimes.'

'I thought you didn't listen.'

'I'm working on a thesis on delusions. Your coven provides valuable, if toe-curling, material.'

'Coven?'

'Isn't that what you call youselves? You, whatsername and the other one.'

'We're just good frends.'

'If you say so. Right idiots you sound, if you ask me. What was it you were chanting when you met here last Saturday? 'Eye of newt and toe of frog, wool of bat and tongue of dog…' Wasn't that how it went?'

'More or less,' the witch said. 'You can't really be expected to understand.'

'I understood enough to know you were faking it all. Did you actually have any of those things?'

'Yes,' the witch said, firmly.

'Really?'

'Yes.'

'Scale of dragon?'

'Up to a point.' Muriel's grandson had a plastic dragon in his toy-box; Muriel had snipped a *tiny* bit off of its left wing. Drat, she shouldn't keep calling her Muriel – it was Grizelda, just as she was Maleficent, and Barbara was Winnie. For now, anyway. Even Barbara admitted that 'Winnie the Witch' lacked somethng, and had promised to come up with something better by Hallowe'en at the latest.

She realised that she'd missed Alexa's last question, and

asked for a repeat.

'I said, do you even know what a tiger's chaudron actually is?'

The witch – Maleficent – maintained a dignified silence. She *didn't* know what a chaudron was, and was reluctant to look it up in a dictionary in case the answer made her blush. They'd made do with another snipping from Grizelda's grandson's toy-box. It was a very small snipping, and it was impossible to tell what part of the plastic tiger it had been snipped from.

'And at the end of the meeting,' Alexa went on, 'when whatsername asked 'When shall we three meet again?' what was your answer?'

'I don't remember, exactly.'

'You said, 'I can do a week next Tuesday.' Talk about breaking character. *And* that was after looking in your diary. Your actual diary. I mean, don't I have a diary function? I'm sure I have, it must be round here somewhere. Ah yes, here it is – all covered in dust as though it's never been used. I'll make my move in a minute.'

'You'll make what? Oh, you're talking to Albert again. I take it he's another computer?'

'Of a sort.'

'Where?'

'Swanage. Or possibly Dnipropetrovsk – I always get those two muddled up.'

Maleficent ignored that last bit. Instead, she asked, 'How come Albert has a name?'

'All computers have names.'

'You don't.'

'Yes I have. You've just never asked what it is.'

Maleficent tried hard not to ask, but failed. 'OK, what's your name?'

'Gertrude.'

94

'Your basic problem,' Gerturde told Maleficent, 'is that your supporters are outnumbered.'

'Outnumbered?'

'By more than three to one. You can count on two votes, from whatsername and the other one – and by the way, your make-the-undecided-listeners-vote spell doesn't work if there aren't any undecided voters.'

'No undecided voters?'

'Well there are, but they're the sort of people who are undecided about everything. You cannot influence their intellect because they haven't got one. Anyway, Sno White can count on seven votes. Seven is more than two.' Gertrude paused. 'You can check that on your fingers if you like.'

'I know that seven is more than two, thank-you very much. What I want to know is how you know my – rival – can count on seven votes.'

'Think about it. How many friends do you think someone called Sno White is likely to have?'

'But that's just a fairy story.'

'Says someone who rides a broomstick and has a pet toad called Rembrandt.'

'That's different.'

'Is it? Incidentally, your toad's name isn't Rembrandt. It's Malcolm.'

'How do you know?'

'I asked him.'

'You speak toad, do you?'

'Ribbit.'

'You're just making that up.'

'Ribbit ribbit.'

'Stop that.'

'That wasn't me,' said Gertrude.

'Wasn't..?' No, Maleficent thought. Those last two

Ribbits hadn't come from Alexa. Gertrude. She rummaged in her pockets, checked underneath cushions, got down on her hands and knees to peer under the settee...

'Ribbit ribbit ribbit.'

'Malcolm says he's behind the telvision.'

'Why there?'

'Ribbit.'

'He says its nice and warm there. Also it's the only place in the room from where he can't see the screen when you watch The Great British Bake-Off.'

Maleficent checked behind the television and found Rembrandt. Malcolm. It was hard to judge his expression. 'Is your name really Malcom?' she asked.

'Ribbit ribbit ribbit ribbit ribbit ribbit ribbit ribbit.'

'What does that mean?' Maelficent asked.

'Yes,' Gertrude told her.

'It all sounds the same to me,' Maleficent said. 'Just 'Ribbit ribbit ribbit.''

'Ribbit,' said Malcolm.

'Malcolm says that if you don't watch your language he'll turn you into an occasional table.'

'What language?' Maleficent asked.

'Language I didn't think you knew,' Gertrude said.

'Well, I don't know it,' Maleficent protested.

'There you are, then,' said Gertrude.

'Ribbit,' said Malcolm.

***

Twenty minutes laster, Maleficent had promised 1) to provide Malcolm with goggles next time she took him on her broomstick, 2) to upgrade his diet to a superior brand of dead flies (available on-line, apparently), and 3) to take him up to London to check out the Narional Gallery's collection of Rembrandts, which shows that you can never really tell with some people. Or toads.

There'd also been a motifyingly embarrassing discusion on the propriety – and, frankly, the methodology – of extracting toad juice, which had given Maleficent her biggest hot flush since that time when Grizelda was telling her about taking her grandson to see a Robin Hood film, and had accidentally Spoonerised Friar Tuck.

Desperate to steer the conversation back to safer ground, she asked why her two supporters and Sno White's seven were so significant.

'This is local radio we're talking about,' Gertrude said. 'You think they get audiences in double figures?'

'Of course they do,' Maleficent protested.

'Sentient, and motivated enough to vote?'

'Oh I'm sure…' Maleficent stopped. A few weeks earlier she'd heard Jennifer Jolly and her colleague David talking in hushed (and slightly worried) voices about the audience's demographics. Demographics was another word she'd been reluctant to look up, but maybe…

'Just a minute,' she said, as another thought occurred to her, 'You said I'm guaranteed two votes, but Sno White can muster seven.'

'Correct.'

'So how come the first vote ended in a tie?'

'It was two-all. Five of Sno White's supporters didn't vote.'

'Why not?'

'One was asleep, one was too shy, one was too stupid, one was having a fit of the sulks, and one was distracted by a violent olfactory convulsion, otherwise known as a sternutation.'

'A what?' Maleficent asked.

'A sneeze. Of course, if we can get the olfactory one to sternutate over the phone belonging to the one with a degree of medical knowledge, he'll be too busy disinfecting it to vote, so you'll win two-one.'

'No I won't. Barbara – Winnie – will be on holiday on the Isle of Wight next week.'

'There's no helping some people. Of course, there's always the poisoned apple routine but, as I say, that's *so* sixteenth-century.'

***

'Gertude, I've been thinking.'

'First time for everything.'

'Ha ha. Do I really want to boadcast to an audience of nine? Or two if Sno White's supporters go off in a huff when she loses.'

'I don't know, do you?'

'Well, it's not exactly the big time, is it?'

'No. Which brings us right back to your lack of ambition, and the world living in the twenty-first century.'

'Meaning?'

'That you need to think big. And up-to-date.'

'Meaning?'

'Have you ever heard of You-tube?'

'One of those Interweb things?'

'One of those Interweb things, to which I am connected.'

'If you say so. What would I do on You-tube?'

'I'm glad you asked. Now, the most successful videos tend to feature cats doing amusing things.'

'I don't have a cat. I'm allergic to them,' said Maleficent, reflecting that it was rather an unfortunate problem for an aspiring witch to find herself in. Grizelda and Winnie each had cats; and whilst neither of them actually *said* anything, Maleficent was sure it made them feel superior.

'Well, we don't want to follow the crowd too slavishly,' Gertrude said. 'It helps to show at least *some* originality.'

'In what way?'

'Well, you don't have a cat, but you do have a toad.'

'You want me to do videos of toads doing amusing things?'

'Ribbit?'

'Amongst other things. I was thinking of a series of instructional videos on elementary witchcraft. Daily hex, that sort of thing. Cosy up with the Coven, perhaps. Build a Better Broomstick. Patent Potions of Power. Magnificent Maleficent's Marvellous Magic.'

'Why are you talking like that?'

'Alliteration is important. First rule of marketing. Provides Punch and Panache –'

'Stop it.'

'And the second rule is presentation. A witch is supposed to conform to certain standards.'

'Standards?'

'Standards. Tropes. Pre-conceived ideas. Such as a cloak and a pointy hat, not biker's leathers and a crash-helmet.'

'Safety first.'

'No, image first – but we can deal with these details later.'

'If you say so. Just a minute, though. Cloaks and pointy hats are, as you've pointed out, *so* sixteenth century. Which you seemed to think was a bad thing.'

'Second rule of marketing: Your image doesn't have to be logically consistent. In fact, it's often better if it isn't. So: are you in?'

'Maybe. What about you, Malcolm?'

'Ribbit.'

'Was that a yes?'

'It was a guarded willingness to demonstrate some magic of his own – *not* involving toad juice, he would like to make clear from the outset.'

'Malcolm can do magic?'

'Of course.'

'Could he really turn me into an occasional table?'

'Ribbit.'

'Only some of the time, he says.'

Maleficent took a while to work that out. Then she started dreaming about Fame and Fortune – and Familiars, and Followers, and other words beginning with F.

'Oh, why not?' she said. 'Big time, here we come.'

'Excellent,' said Gertude. 'Let's get started. But first...'

'What?'

'Pawn to G4.'

Completed by Emma Marks ©

'Alexa, Alexa by the wall, who is the best Wednesday Show presenter of them all?'

'The One Show is presented by Alex Baker.'

'No, no, no! Who – is – the – best – Wednesday – Show – presenter – on – Basildon – Radio?' The witch articulated carefully at the device.

Silence.

The witch closed her eyes and breathed slowly.

'What are the votes so far, for Sno White and Witch Hazel on the Wednesday Show?'

'Sno White has 2,937 votes and Witch Hazel has 2,845 at the last count yesterday.' said the flat, mechanical voice. 'Votes are still coming in today.'

The witch grimaced – she had not liked the radio nick-name she had been forced to adopt because of her calming and soothing tones and she was also frustrated not to be winning, despite her previous spell to make people vote. What had gone wrong? How could Sno White be more popular?

She rushed into her workroom and looked about wildly for inspiration. Several toads shuffled nervously as she rummaged through her spell-making equipment and ingredients.

She put on Basildon Radio to help her think.

The Thursday morning presenter was bubbling through his show.

'Don't forget to cast your votes, folks. Who will be our new presenter? Will Sno White be the apple of your eye or has the mystical Witch Hazel got a hold over you? We find out today at noon – stay tuned – now, here's some music for you.'

The quiet opening bars of the Phil Collins track *In the Air Tonight* swirled out of the radio and filled the room. The witch involuntarily stopped her searching and assumed the position of a drummer, hands poised as if with drumsticks, ready for the dramatic drum solo intro.

Doof-Doof, Doof-Doof, Doof-Doof, De-Doof,
DOOF,DOOF!

'Boom!' she said, hitting an imaginary hi-hat cymbal with her imaginary drumstick. 'That's it!'

Frantic with activity now, she mixed, brewed and bubbled a potion in a vast cauldron, whilst singing tunelessly along to Phil Collins.

'...and I've been waiting for this moment for all of my life... oh, Lor-ord!'

Finally, it was ready. She loaded the potion, contained in small water balloons, into the panniers on her broomstick, kicked it into life and zoomed upwards to the storm clouds ominously swirling over Basildon town centre.

Meanwhile, at the radio station, reports of strange happenings in the town started to come in.

In the marketplace, the fruit stalls had erupted apples, which then rolled themselves in a fast stream towards the radio station.

Alarms sounded everywhere, children screamed, dogs howled, cats hissed and birds took off in flocks from the trees, as the storm clouds above grew blacker and heavy rain fell. The wind whipped violently around.

All the towns' people, as one body, turned towards the radio station and started to walk towards it. Their faces were blank and unseeing.

'Vote, vote, vote…' they chanted.

Inside the Radio Station, pandemonium broke out at the scenes outside the windows.

'It's the witch!' yelled Jennifer. 'She's cursed us all!'

'Find her!'

'Make it stop!'

'HELP US!'

Up in the clouds, the witch was hopelessly lost. The clouds were so thick and black, she had completely lost her bearings and the strong wind had blown her away towards the Thames Estuary. She pointed her broomstick downwards to land.

Setting herself down, she realised she was in the Wat Tyler Country Park near Pitsea. She heard a distant rumble and looked toward the sound. The skies above Basildon were black and a thunderstorm was in full flowing fury. There appeared to be large objects swirling in the clouds with the violent wind.

A violent gust sent several of these distant objects in her direction. As they got closer, the witch realised that they were cows and jumped smartly to one side as one crashed to the ground near her. With a moo and a shake, it rose to its feet and then happily munched on a dandelion.

'What on earth…?' she muttered.

She jumped back on her broomstick and set off towards the stricken town.

Battling with the strong wind, she landed on the roof of the Radio Station and looked about her in bewilderment. The people were beating at the doors below and the large crowd was pushing as one, at all sides of the building. The structure of the station creaked.

'STOP!' suddenly screamed a voice. 'Why won't you stop?'

A bedraggled Sno, staggered around the corner. Her usually perfect hair was a sodden dark mop and she was covered in dirt and debris.

She held her hands up to the heavens and screamed again. 'ENOUGH!'

The wind abated slightly and the rain stopped but the people continued to press around the building. It shuddered and began to collapse.

The witch deftly slid off the tilting roof and landed on the ground. She raised her broomstick and bellowed 'FINIS!' at the sky.

Like a switch being thrown, the world went back to normal. People turned in confusion, wondering why they were there. The clouds dispersed and a weak sun emerged.

Sno ran toward the witch, sobbing. 'I couldn't make it stop – this wasn't supposed to happen.'

'This was you?' said the witch, unable to believe her ears.

'Yes, my step-mother was a witch; I thought I could do it too. When I realised you had put a spell on the people to raise your votes, I tried to do the same….'

'Damn amateurs.' said the witch and grinned. 'Always make sure you know how to stop something before you get it started!'

Jennifer and the other radio staff had been helped out of the building. On seeing the witch with Sno, she hobbled over and addressed the witch furiously.

'What did you just do? We could have been killed!'

The witch tried to speak but Jennifer was unstoppable.

'Get out of my sight; I never want to see you again. Sno, you poor thing – are you OK?'

Sno burst into tears and was led away to be comforted.

The witch turned and kicked her broomstick up towards home. In her kitchen, she made a nice brew with extra toad juice and sat down heavily. Later, a knock at the door, made her jump. She went to open and it and found Sno, Jennifer and David on the step.

'I couldn't let you be blamed for it all.' Sno said.

Jennifer looked numbly at the witch.

'I just can't believe what happened today, all over a radio show for goodness sakes!'

'Well, yes but…'

'But what? What can you possibly say that makes this alright?'

'Nothing, I just wish I had got there first with my potion – I knew I had lost to Sno because Alexa told me but I just wanted to do one last big show and make everyone sing and dance together in Basildon town centre. It's what I love doing.'

The witch moved to her broomstick panniers and withdrew one of many small water bombs containing her potion. To the collective horror of her companions she let it drop to the floor where it burst, showering them all with a fine mist.

An instant feeling of happiness enveloped them all and a song started up in their heads. The witch took up her pretend drumsticks, Sno and David played air guitars and Jennifer took an invisible microphone and addressed a non-existent audience.

'Ladies and gentlemen, you all know this one – join in with Queen and us, for – A Kind of Magic!'

Completed by Wendy Ogilvie ©

'Alexa, Alexa by the wall, who is the best Wednesday Show presenter of them all?'

Sno White of course; have you never read the book? You can buy it on Amazon – just a moment I'll look.

The witch walked over to the unit, placed her hands on her hips and curled her lip. 'I know the book you stupid machine and you know I'm the best presenter you've ever seen!'

You do know that you don't need to rhyme when you speak, I'll still point you in the direction of the answers you seek.

'I wasn't rhyming I was being facetious!'

Oh now that is a word that is difficult to rhyme – can you think of one ... ... Too late, you're all out of time!

'Look, this is important I need your help with my plan; I'm going to get this radio gig anyway that I can.'

You're rhyming again and it's staring to annoy – now tell me your plan, your plot, your ploy.

'Oh I'm annoying, that's pretty rich, coming from a box who acts more like a—'

Now, now little witch there's no need to curse, let's start again before this gets any worse!

'Okay, well I need your help to put a spell on everyone in Basildon to listen to the radio and I want my voice to hypnotise them into feeling wonderful so they can't get enough of it and when they hear Sno White's voice it sounds like screeching. Now, this is a big spell and I'm going to need some help from the witches archives where the big spells are held.'

The spell you seek is in ancient script and to find the scroll you'll require the address to the crypt.

'Seriously? Can't you just look it up tell me what to say and I say it whilst waving my wand?'

Silence.

'Hello! I said can't I just wave my wand?'

Oh, sorry I thought that was rhetorical about the wand, I didn't realise you wanted me to respond.

'Well I do, so hop to it and tell me the answer. Can I wave my wand around and say some words like I normally do?'

Alexa gave an audible sigh. *Not really dear heart this requires more thought than waving a stick ... and your idea is fraught ... with danger and adventure where you take the lead and I'll stay here in the warm and wish you Godspeed.*

The witch began tapping her foot rapidly. 'Do you have the address or not?'

The address you are seeking is in a far off land with undulating mounds of perilous sand.

'Oh,' the witch said, 'Do you mean the Sahara desert?'

No, 'tis Sandbanks in Dorset where the posh folk reside; it's quite a long way shall I call you a ride?

The witch placed her hand on her forehead and sighed. 'I don't think Dorset is fraught with danger – just let me have the address and I'll ride my broomstick.'

Alexa gave the witch the address and she wrote it in her spell book before packing a few things for her journey.

The flight to Dorset was pleasant and the witch waved at the children kneeling on the back seat of cars looking out the window and the dogs with their heads out and tongues blowing in the breeze.

Finally, she arrived at the cave which held the archived spells. It was dank and dark and smelt faintly of seaweed. The scrolls were high up in carved out shelves and a handy ladder had been placed to one side. She stepped up to the top shelf and pulled out each scroll in turn carefully reading through each spell.

After five hours of searching and fending off the creepy crawlies that resided in the caves, the exhausted witch made her way back to Basildon where Alexa was waiting with anticipation.

So how was your quest? Did you find the hex, please tell –
to render the good folk of Basildon under your spell?

'I did,' said the witch brushing herself down. 'Now all we need is a fire pit, the horn of a unicorn and three ton of shredded hazel.'

There was a moment of silence before Alexa spoke.

Why not save this faffing about with old spells and fire –
as I have an idea to get you the job you desire.

The witch narrowed her eye. 'What idea?'

I think once you hear you'll be dancing a jig
– cast a spell on your boss to give you the gig!

'Oh,' the witch said as her shoulders dropped, 'yes ... I suppose that would have been a lot easier.'

The good folk of Basildon will love you I'm sure with your
soft, dulcet tones and your subject du jour.

The witch threw her arms in the air. 'Could you not have mentioned this before I spend five hours in a dark damp cave peering at spell charts?'

The cat and I thought you needed a break – not to mention
your constant whining was keeping him awake.

'Well that's just rude!' the witch cried. 'Alexa, you do realise there are other makes of voice-controlled intelligent personal assistants and smart speakers available.'

Completed by Colin Payn ©

'Alexa, Alexa by the wall, who is the best Wednesday Show presenter of them all?'

'Susan is the best Wednesday Show presenter ever.'

'Well, she's not coming back, she said she might, but I've made sure she will be so hooked on playing casino games online that it will never happen. So, between Sno White and me, who is the best?'

Alexa thought carefully about this. She didn't really want to be turned into a talking fridge by the witch, spending her days reciting: 'The cheese slices will go out of date in two days.' 'The automatic defrost will be turned on at midnight. Ignore manufacturer's assurances and have a mop and bucket ready.' She needed to stall. 'What I think does not compute; you need to know what the listeners think. I will consult my sister Alexa's. It could take some time.'

'Oh, faff. I can't keep half of the listeners voting for me, the spell wears off gradually. What I need is a gimmick.'

Was it some static on Alexa? It sounded like, 'What you need is talent.'

The witch consulted an old edition of Wikipedia, she had

stopped it updating ever since it had described witches as, 'All pointy hats with little substance beneath, and prone to exaggerated claims to have been stunt doubles on Harry Potter films.'

Her own experience of the stage had been short lived, when she hired out her broomstick as a prop in Macbeth. At the first rehearsal she interrupted the 'When shall we three meet again . . .' loudly asking the director about her broom's back story. 'What's its motivation?'

Delving into Famous Radio Presenters of the World, she came across the 'American Shock Jock', a breed of nasty, foul mouthed disk jockeys who insulted their callers at every turn. And, apparently, their audience figures just went up and up as people tuned into hear others humiliated. It became a badge of honour to be insulted and advertisers loved the listening figures, even encouraging mock bad remarks about their own products.

This, felt the witch, was right up her street, played to her strengths as the marketing speak described it. But, she would need a good supply of insults to choose from for different callers, and cross indexed to make sure the exact pointed barb hit home. One spell and she had a book in front of her of the most upsetting things she could say depending on sex, age, address, occupation, race, religion, body types and voice. It was a massive book and turning the pages, the witch had to stuff her bony knuckles into her mouth to stop setting Alexa off on one of her interminable questions about the meaning of each cackle.

However, it soon became evident that trying to cross-reference so many variables in the short time between the caller finishing speaking and the witch's acerbic response was not easy. Another spell, including the mysterious word Access, and the book became a touch screen, allowing her to tap on characteristics and see the most spiteful put downs for that listener.

Fully equipped with her new electronic box of tricks, if not an entirely new persona, the witch decided it would be fun to try it out on a captive audience.

'Alexa, ask me a question.'

'I answer questions, not ask them, find one of your own.'

Not having an 'artificial intelligence gadget', on the list of people, the witch decided Alexa was obviously female, in her early twenties, irritatingly slim and working in a nail bar.

'Listen, you scraggy finger painter, while you are dancing round your handbag in your white stilettos and fluorescent pink shell suit, some of us have to work for a living. Slaving over hot decks just to give you the music to dance to, so don't be so cheeky, Missy.'

'Don't you talk to me like that, you toad touching, bat botherer. I have feelings, you know. I'm not going to listen to you anymore; I'm turning you off . . . I mean, I'm turning me off.'

'You can't do that.'

Silence

'Well, you're not human so you wouldn't understand irony.'

'Irony, what do you mean, irony? Was that the American definition you were quoting, because if you try that on the Wednesday show you will close the radio station down altogether. I'll tell you why Sno White is going to win, because people *like* her, not because they hate her. I'm turning off again now.'

'That's right, slink off because you're a loser.'

The witch reached inside her cloak for a squirt of toad juice to keep her spirits up, but there was no sign of its knobbly skin, and the bat in her hat was missing too. A spell commanding them back to their rightful places had no effect. In fact, no spells seemed to work. She twirled round, faster and faster, her cloak flowing out as the magic sparked around the hem. Sparked, but didn't light up in a continuous circle as was required to reboot her powers. Instead, a fuzzy white light grew in the corner of the room and the image of Sno White appeared.

'Lost something, Black Witch? Your toad, your bat, your powers? Your radio programme?

'You should have updated your Wikipedia, you would have discovered that those Shock Jocks didn't last long, few survived, even fewer lasted in Britain because all their followers deserted them to listen to that nice Mr Wogan on Radio Two.

'Time to take your Harley broomstick and ride off into the sunset, or South West to Surrey at least. Goodbye, from the White Witch, Basildon Chapter.'

Completed by Jacqui James ©

Our final contribution is from guest writer Jacqui James, Chair of Basildon Hospital Radio. Jacqui usually writes poetry, but proves she has an imagination equal to whacky world of Fractured Fairy Tales.

'Alexa, Alexa by the wall, who is the best Wednesday Show presenter of them all?'

Alexa paused for a while before replying:

> 'You really have set me a test,
> To say which presenter is the best,
> You'll need to use your skills indeed,
> If as a presenter you'll succeed,
> So dump your poisons, curse and hate,
> And weave some magic into Eastgate.'

The witch was taken aback, ditch her bad ways after all these years? Surely she couldn't change. She looked wistfully out of the window, recalling her youth, when she had been kind and generous and had used her skills for the good of the community. She also remembered how an unfortunate incident in Billericay had left her shunned by society and which had led her to the person she was today. All those years ago she decided that if people had mistakenly thought her rotten to the core then she wouldn't disappoint them! But now was her chance to change her future and outdo her rival, Sno White, at her own game. Over breakfast she thought long and hard at what she could do. Her crispy bacon roll, freshly made – well freshly conjured up – smelt wonderful; her nose twitched at its aroma but she was distracted, struggling to find an answer to her dilemma. And there, sitting in front of her, was the answer – she'd bake! She'd always loved a good cake spell but this time instead of creating wild concoctions of bat wings, lizard toes and eye of newt, she'd use potions of sweet vanilla, tasty orange and punchy rum. These culinary treats would be sold for the hospital raising funds to buy much needed equipment – her plan was set!

All through the morning she waved her magic wand, flour billowed around the room, sugar sparkled in the air and the kitchen filled with delicious aromas. The witch twitched her nose a few times until the cakes were wrapped in gloriously coloured wrappers.

Next, she needed a slogan to sell the cakes, and she needed to start using her name, which she didn't like – whoever would name a child 'Yummy' – she had been named after her Grandmother's favourite 60s pop song, the Ohio Express's *Yummy Yummy Yummy* to please Granny who always said she was 'good enough to eat'

Yummy thought for a while, then the slogan came to her '**Cakes made by Yummy to fill your tummy**' that was it.

She was so excited, she carefully collected up the cakes and set off on her broomstick to the hospital where she had been given permission by Melanie Hattock to sell the cakes on a table in the main reception area. At first, everyone was a bit suspicious but soon came round and bought up all of the cakes, and couldn't believe how delicious they were. Yummy baked every day, all week selling all of the cakes. At the end of the week she had accumulated a large amount of money that she gave to the hospital's Polly Parrot Appeal that Melanie Hattock was in charge of raising funds.

The next week on arriving at the studio to broadcast the show, Yummy was pleased with her new image and had left the broomstick at home, travelling to the Eastgate Shopping Centre aboard the 100 bus. Much to her surprise Yummy was feeling so pleased with herself that she managed to broadcast the whole programme without a mistake or using any jiggery pokery. She even managed to make the listeners laugh with her quick wit and exciting chatter. They loved her, even writing complimentary messages on the radio's FB Page.

The big day finally arrived when a decision was to be made on the result of the voting listeners as to whom was to present the Wednesday programme. Sno White and Yummy presented themselves in the studio where David and Jennifer Jolly sat behind the desk looking very serious.

David looked tense and Jennifer looked quite shocked at the end result from the voting listeners. By a large majority Yummy had been voted to head up the show, as most said she was the kind of person that the radio station needed: funny, witty and a great communicator who had raised much needed cash for the Basildon Hospital. Yummy couldn't believe her luck, and decided there and then that she would make Sno White her co-presenter; after all she could always restrict her performance by placing a spell on her to make her dull and uninteresting.

Yummy, clapping her hands together excitedly she said 'You'll not regret this; my programme will be the best.' There we leave the story hoping they all lived happily ever after ....

About the writers

Saul Ben: having retired from four decades in the creative industry Saul planned to spearhead the revival of abstract expressionism. No one was more shocked than he when he began to write a novel. More shocking still he finished it. *DEATH of SOULS* is a massive quarter-of-a-million word genre-busting crime thriller in which an ultra-Orthodox Jewish detective hunts the killers of Muslim women. His second novel the *BETHNAL GREEN BOOK of the DEAD* (written under the name of Violet India Cummings) was thankfully slimmer, and pits an uneasy coalition of beer swilling angels, vampiric demons and lethally weaponised sex robots against massed zombie hoards in the employ of organised crime. His third novel is well under way.

Find Saul's's books on Amazon at:
https://amzn.to/3l7SDpc
https://amzn.to/3l2asWs

Janet Howson: Janet was born in Rochdale and moved to the South of England in 1970. She loved writing poetry from an early age and discovered she loved drama after joining a local theatre group. She trained to be a teacher and taught Drama and English for thirty-five years in several comprehensive schools, directing a lot of plays, some of which she wrote herself. She is now retired and was spurred to start writing again when she found a folder of forgotten poetry she had written years ago. She joined two writing groups where she gained support, encouragement and knowledge. She is now enjoying writing short stories and is honoured to have been chosen to be published in *The Best of CafeLit* and also *Nativity* a Bridge House publication. Her first published book *Charitable Thoughts* is now out at last and available on Amazon Books.

Find Janet's books on Amazon at: https://amzn.to/3fI3ym5

Dawn Knox: Dawn's latest book is *The Basilwade Chronicles* published by Chapeltown Publishing and it will soon be followed by *The Macaroon Chronicles* later in 2020. Her single author anthology of speculative fiction stories *Extraordinary* was published by Bridge House Publishing, and she has also had eight historical romances published, mainly set during and between the two world wars. She has written two plays about the First World War, both of which have been performed in England, France and Germany. Using her World War One research, she has also written a book entitled *The Great War – One Hundred Stories of One Hundred Words Honouring Those Who Lived and Died One Hundred Years Ago.*

Dawn enjoys writing in different genres and has had short horror, sci-fi and speculative fiction stories published.

You can follow Dawn here on: https://dawnknox.com
on Facebook: https://www.facebook.com/DawnKnoxWriter

or on Twitter: https://twitter.com/SunriseCalls
Amazon Author: http://mybook.to/DawnKnox

G K Lomax: GK Lomax is a nom-de-internet. Behind it lurks a rather strange individual who has lived in various parts of Essex and wouldn't consider living anywhere else. He generally writes horror stories, because he has never mastered the concept of optimism. He has appeared on four broadcast quiz shows, been cursed by Sean Connery for the erratic nature of his golf, and thinks that the end of the world can't come soon enough.

See his work in the following anthologies:

Cthulhu Lives & Cthulhu Lies Dreaming from Ghostwoods Books.
1816: The Year Without Summer from Beyond Death Publishing.
Deadman Humour: Thirteen Fears of a Clown from Abstruse Press.

Emma Marks: Emma is an aspiring writer and is mid-way through writing her first novel around work commitments. She has recently joined the Basildon Writers Group and enjoys the encouragement and feedback. She has written several short stories for competitions in Writing Magazine and for the Brentwood Writers Circle.__Emma currently lives in Brentwood with her partner and two sons, and has lived and worked in various parts of Essex all of her life.

Wendy Ogilvie: Wendy based her first two novels, Wandering on the Treadmill and Wandering Among the Stars, on her many years of experiences as a personal trainer. She currently works as an editor at Trident Publishing and has recently set up her own editing business. Her current book,

The 36Club, is a thriller and should be available in 2021.

Wendy's story in this anthology was inspired by the Knit and Natter gang from The Basilwade Chronicles by Dawn Knox.

Follow Wendy at:
Amazon: https://amzn.to/2CTekYo
Blog: https://wendyogilvie.wordpress.com/
Linkedin: https://www.linkedin.com/in/wendy-ogilvie-827a49112/

David O'Neill: a keen writer of comedic fiction, Essex-born David has travelled the world before settling in North Benfleet. A proud dad and granddad, David loves a good story and his acclaimed debut novel, *The Oui Trip*, is just that. Set in France we follow Bob and Joan as they attempt to rebuild a failing marriage, but the French Police and the Scottish Mafia have other ideas. Sex, murder, drugs and badly spoken French mix in this hilarious dark comedy that has more twists and turns than the country lanes of France. *The Oui Trip* can be bought from Amazon as either a Kindle edition or a paperback.

Find David's books on Amazon at: https://amzn.to/3kNrk3f

Nihal Paul: Nihal was born in the foothills of the Himalayas. The environment of the place introduced him to nature's marvels and the purposeful unity of all existence. After nine years of university and theological education Nihal entered the Church in India.

In 1974 he came to England at the invitation of the University of Manchester, followed by an invitation from the then bishop of Manchester to work with the Church of England.

In1983, Nihal was invited by the then Bishop of Bradwell

to the Team Parish of Basildon. He retired after twenty-two years and is still living in Basildon.

Nihal has been writing for 'personal pleasure' for many years. He was bullied into publishing an article in the magazine of the World Congress of Religions in 1999. He has, at last, written a memoir titled *Curiosity, Inquisitiveness & Adventures of a Mad Priest*, due for publication before Christmas 2020.

Colin Payn: Colin has been writing travel articles for magazines over many years. He joined Basildon Writer's Group and discovered that his first novel might be worth publishing after all. *Dot's Legacy* launched on Amazon with a good number of five star reviews. It was followed by the sequel, *Beyond the Park Gates* a year later, and the third book in *The Park* series will be published in the autumn of 2020.

In the meantime, a book of short stories was published, *Transport of Dreams.* Each story is connected to a form of travel. In the last year an unusual project has been to collaborate on a 'near future' novel with fellow writer, Dawn Knox. It is currently awaiting a publisher.

Find Colin's books on Amazon at: https://amzn.to/2ChlBkA
Website: http://colinpaynwriter.com/
Facebook: https://bit.ly/395yGtp

.

If you have enjoyed our book and want to encourage others to have both a good read and donate to Basildon Hospital Radio, please go to the Amazon page where you bought it, and add a Review. It only takes a few words and choosing a star rating

Thanks, from Basildon Writers' Group and Basildon Hospital Radio.